BITCH'N

A.J. Converse

1

BITCH'N

Dedication

To my wife of 44 years, Melinda, for her consideration all these years and especially her love, help, support and patience during the long hours of editing and re-editing this novel.

A. J. Converse

BITCH'N

1

Wednesday July 6, 1960

God, the cops just walked up to pop as he checked the points on our '57 Ford Fairlane. I could see them from the front room window. Every little detail, the tuft of Bermuda grass growing through the crack in the asphalt, the motion of the palm leaves at the top of the trees surrounding the tenants' parking, the cloudless sky, all froze as if time itself stopped when the cops stood in front of Pop.

Pop rose scowling and closed the hood. I heard the cop's voice.

"We want to see Herman."

Pop raised his voice, the way he chewed out sailors. "What the hell do you want with my son after all the other stuff?"

The cop's legs stiffened. He folded his arms. "We want to ask him a few questions."

I moved closer to the window, straining to hear. *Nothing happened in the weeks since Joe Carlson's murder. Why...now...new evidence? What could it be...?*

I heard the word "ashtray."

The ashtray - that must be it. I hit Carlson with the ashtray stand before I finished him. I lived in fear of the authorities somehow connecting it to me.

Mom walked into the room and stood next to me at the window. "What's going on?"

I stared through the window. A smudge of grey where the lawn sprinklers had hit the window, leaving a slick of moisture that accumulated dust and then dried, streaked the lower portion of the window. I stared at it, trying to still the fear.

"I think they're talking to pop about me," I said.

I tried to keep my voice steady. My secret screamed at my conscious. Like I'd felt standing on the edge of Hoover Dam on one of our vacation car trips; the pull of the view to the bottom made my legs weak. Just as the terrible draw at the precipice tugged at me then, I feared blurting out the truth. Knowing that Mom didn't know didn't calm me.

"Not that drug business again, I hope," Mom said.

She headed for the door to our little duplex. I watched her walk out to where they stood. She walked as if chilly, with her arms folded. The July afternoon sun in Coronado shined warm, not hot. The weatherman called it balmy.

"We just want his fingerprints..." I heard the cops say. The rest I couldn't hear.

Pop sputtered. "You're crazy if you think my son had anything to do with it. How many prints were on that ashtray, anyway – a thousand, I bet. That Carlson kid and his Mexican friends nearly killed my son. Leave him alone."

The cops looked at each other and shrugged. "Okay, we'll have to tell the chief you won't cooperate."

Pop leaned into them, his face inches from theirs. "Get the hell out of here. You don't have any business bothering my family." I could see the veins in his neck even from my side of the window.

"Tell your chief that."

Mom grabbed his arm, easing him away. He glared at the two cops as they backed away. "Tell him that," he repeated. The cops withdrew to their car.

Shit, were they on to me?

Pop stood up for me. That was just the way he was. How could I ever justify what I did? Mom, how could I tell her? They believed in my honesty. They trusted their son. Mom and Pop could never imagine that I would do such a thing...and not tell them... I would have told them. Their child, a good kid, not a murderer... in their minds, the cops had no business bothering me in the first place. My agreement to testify against Carlson put my life in danger, and now the cops accused me of killing him - no, not their son, never.

I couldn't imagine my life if anyone found out that I murdered Joe Carlson - no matter the circumstances. It must stay a secret. My thing with Liz, my plans for college, everything, gone if ever anyone found out. *Thank God, they couldn't read my mind.*

If only I could live the year over. It had started out bitch'n.

A. J. Converse

2

1959

I showed off a little with that last wave, hoping the chicks would notice this sophomore stud in the surf. Finishing near the shore, I found myself off to the right of my buddies gathered on the sand. I rose, standing waist deep in the water directly in front of the five voluptuous senior girls we had dubbed the *big five.* The warm water of Southern California's late summer enticed me to linger in the shallow water and take in the view.

It's funny how I could always notice even a slight flaw in a single chick, but when I encountered a group of girls on the street or on the beach, their collective sexiness seemed to wash out all individual imperfections. If one had a too-large mouth or another crooked teeth it didn't register. The charms of all seemed to blend into one image of perfection in my mind. The big five hung out together so often that my mental image of each had been altered. Each took on the aura of an angel. They created the same effect on my buddies.

Jill Hankins stretched out to retrieve the vinegar and iodine concoction for her skin. That I knew, didn't work to prevent sunburn. Nothing worked except the gradual building up of a tan. I watched her stretch out. What the hell, she could use vinegar and iodine as much as she wanted.

Shaking off my reverie, I examined them separately. Katie Gutierrez displayed a voluptuous body in a too small maroon bikini. Her rich Spaniard parents lived in one of

7

the Coronado beach mansions. The rest owed their presence in Coronado to their Navy fathers. Sue Pricy's one-piece suit helped hide her slight chubbiness. Its low cut front showed a deep cleavage and luscious tits. Sharon Galloway's hot pink, two-piece suit showed off her figure and her long dark blond hair. Jillian jiggled in her sky blue two-piece bathing suit, the old style, not a bikini. And Liz Edgerton ...aww Liz... sat upright, her yellow bikini advertising her untouchable body. A devout Christian, her long slim shape included with out doubt, the best ass in Christendom.

The lifeguards moved the red flag while I stared at the chicks. I missed it. Showing off, I turned back toward the open water and jumped up over an incoming wave. I ignored the undertow and swam out toward the bigger swells. I plunged under the crash of breakers. I wanted to reach the one perfect large rolling swell before it broke. The churning surf and undertow started to slow me, but I wanted to impress the big five. I forced my way out. The water pulled me out faster, too fast. I struggled. The water's power grew. What happened? I don't know, but shit; now I was in trouble. My stomach tightened. I could drown. *Get it together.*

The green water pulled me further toward the open sea. Flapping shards of seaweed grasped at my legs. A memory of a long past Phys Ed. swimming lecture on what to do in a riptide popped into my head. *Swim at right angles to the shore.* That old lecture seemed pointless. As the waves moved through the rip, they churned instead of breaking normally. I sputtered with mouthfuls of salt water as the surges dunked me again and again. The nose-full did it. All I needed now was a cramp.

I spotted a lifeguard on the sand moving toward my part of the beach. He stared at me. The big five sat up, looking at me. I might drown if the lifeguard doesn't rescue me, but then shit, the big five would see him rescue me. *Calm down, think.* Trying to appear cool, I stopped flailing my arms. I didn't want any lifeguard swimming out to rescue me. I'm tough I told myself, stifling an urge to call for help. I could see the other lifeguard approaching with his float. The chicks and my friends stared out me.

I always thought myself a strong swimmer, but body surfing and fighting a rip current were two different things. I forgot the old advice to swim at right angles to the rip. Taking a chance, I lunged toward shore as each wave crashed around me. Using the waves to over-come the current, I made some progress toward the beach. The churning breakers still provided some forward momentum. I tapped that momentum.

The lifeguards moved out waist deep watching me. I concentrated on appearing calm and deliberate. My feet finally touched bottom.

Thank God.

My heart pounded from the exertion. I avoided the rip. I avoided the humiliation of rescue. My lungs burned. I tried to look cool and in control as I walked my way out of the water. Reaching sand, I bent over and put my hands on my knees to catch my breath. The lifeguards strode up to me.

"What the hell were you doing out there? Didn't you see the red flag?" One of them yelled at me - nothing like a pissed-off ex-frogman to make your day at the beach. That's how the city got its lifeguards – ex-frogmen.

Fuck you, trying to look big in front of the chicks, I thought.

Trying to act calm, I said, "I've been in the water for a couple of hours. I didn't see you move the flag, sorry."

"Well, stay out of the water it's treacherous." He said.

Trying not to puff, I walked up the beach with as much nonchalance as I could fake. Then I flopped down in the sand between my buddies and the chicks.

"Don't you have a towel?" Liz Edgerton said.

She looked at me through lidded eyes as she spoke, her slim finger on her chin, one of the big five. Bitch'n.

***

Liz found herself talking to him. She first noticed him a couple of years before, when as a sophomore she saw him playing Pony League Baseball. A certain maturity about his mannerisms appealed to her. His body had firmed up more since then, making him even more attractive. He was average size for a high school boy but his body seemed harder, like that of a young adult. His light brown hair hung nearly to his eyes. Another patch of hair ran down his belly into his cutoffs. It drew her eyes. Was he aware that she was not much older than he?

***

"Hey, what'd the life guard say to you Mo? He looked pissed." Jon said.

The guys call me Mo.

I ignored Jon and said to Liz, "No, I never use a towel; I just lie in the sand 'til I'm dry."

"Oh ... I was gonna offer to dry you off with my towel."

She curled her long legs under her bottom and sat up straight, pushing her hands straight down on the sand, emphasizing the curve of the small of her back. I wished that I could dust off the sand particles that clung to her yellow bikini bottom.

"You're welcome to dry me off anytime, Liz. You can do it now if you want."

She giggled. "You would like that, I bet."

***

She stopped herself there. Boys could be like quicksand, her mom warned her many times. They could ruin her future if she allowed her feelings to control her. Keep a tight control of her feelings until she was older, her mom preached. Liz's mind filled with forbidden urges so she forced herself to stop flirting and turned briskly to talk to Katie, tossing her hair provocatively over her shoulder.

***

I turned to look at my gawking friends. Between Jon and Rich sat a small cooler with an open lid. Jon Jackman

11

sipped on a beer. His older brother probably bought a six-pack for him. He sometimes acted as a tap for the guys.

Hampton McCarty sat next to Jon with his shades on, looking cool. He had something in a paper cup, probably scotch from his father's liquor cabinet. He liked to replace the scotch he pilfered with tap water. The guys wondered just how much watering down the bottle could handle before the old man discovered it.

Rich Lévesque lounged laconically on his elbows.

Larson Burke sat next to Rich with his arms on his knees, grinning at the girls foolishly. He could look square just sitting there.

"So what's the haps?" I said. Everyone in the school said haps for happening. I came to the beach early to get in some surfing. I had to get home in the afternoon to fix my motorbike for my paper route in the morning. The guys came later. We planned to hit the last beach party of the summer in the evening.

"Aw, we had to wait for Larson to finish mowing his parent's lawn. We sat around his patio for half the morning teasing his sister.

"How about hanging around," Jon said.

Then he raised his voice, looking at the girls, "We can see if the chicks wanna ride around town with us"

Jillian yelled back, "How'd we all fit in that dinky old car of Rich's?"

"No problem," Jon said, "You can sit on our laps."

"Or take turns in the back seat," Rich said under his breath.

Jillian heard it and chimed in, "Only in your dreams, Daddy-O. Never send a boy to do a man's job, I always say."

The chicks all laughed. They knew who we were and we knew who they were, but hey, they were the big five. We'd never talked to them before. Now that we had some banter going with them and on the beach too, I had to leave. *Crap*.

I turned to Jon and said, "I gotta get back and fix my motorbike for my route tomorrow."

"You're getting as square as Larson, Mo. Don't you know it's not cool to have a paper route in high school. Kids deliver papers. Hell Mo, now we're sophomores."

"Hey, I don't have rich parents to give me bread like you Jon, if I want wheels I gotta pay for the car myself. That's why I'm working. Anyway it gives me beer money."

"Aww, you don't drink enough beer to get a girl high. Mo." Jon said.

"I wanna play football this year, not just sit on the bench like last year. I don't need to get caught by the beach patrol and get kicked off the team. Then there's Mom. She'd have a conniption and convince Pop to ground me forever if I got arrested.   If I got drunk like you and

13

Hampton, the beach patrol might catch me. A little high, I still can run fast."

"You're a pussy. Anyway we never get caught." Jon said.

"Hey watch that," Jillian shouted at Jon. "There are ladies present."

"Huh, where are the ladies?" Rich said, looking around as if he was really searching for some.

Jillian got up, came over, and threw a paper cup of soda on him. I hated to leave, things were getting fun.

"I'd like to hang out with you guys some more, but I gotta split." I said as I stood up and pulled on my old sweatshirt, and shuffled into my go-aheads.

What passed for the town hoods strode up acting like junior high kids. Their swagger marked them as big-shot seniors. Stan Huffman led the way. Big, blond, white and fat, he played backup fullback on the football team the previous year. If he didn't get his ass kicked out of school, he might be first string this year. He thought that he was a big stud. He brushed his crew-cut blond hair sides back to a duck-ass. He wore dark levies tuned under at the cuffs so as not to show the seam or the turn-up. In 1959, guys never wore faded Levis. Since Levis faded as soon as they were washed, cool cats rarely washed them. His too-small white t-shirt made him look ridiculous with his baby fat. To cap off his hard-guy look, he sported a cigarette pack rolled up in one sleeve. He affected the TJ look of Mexican sandals died black and worn over white sweat socks. The sandals came only from Mexico. They consisted of un-dyed leather straps on cheap soles made of rubber from old tires. We called them Huaraches. If you wore them, ostensibly you hung out in Tijuana. Except in Stan's case, his mom probably picked them up during one of her shopping trips. Privileged captain's kids like him filled Coronado. He normally got As and Bs in school. He inherited his parents' brains, not their common sense. Stan's naïveté made him appear plain stupid sometimes.

He usually hung with four other pseudo hoods of privileged backgrounds. Two stood with him now, Del Webber, a slight kid with blond hair, brushed back in a DA, with the standard dark Levis and white t-shirt, sort of a miniature Stan, and Joe Carlson.

Joe Carlson liked to fight. Anger filled him for some reason. A skinny, greasy bastard, he combed his black hair into a duck-ass pompadour. He carried a knife. He liked to come up behind freshman boys and hit them on the tops of their heads with his knuckle when walking the school's halls. Carlson scared me.

Stan struck a pose in front of me and said, "What are you assholes doing talking to senior chicks?"

A knot of fear-rage tightened my abdomen. I pointed at his feet.

"Bitch'n sandals Stanley. Did your Mommy buy them for you in Mexico?"

I heard Rich mutter, "Huh oh."

The guys sat up at attention. They could see what was coming. They knew that if I had to fight I would, and they might get into it too. None of us wanted this day at the beach to end in a fight. Flirting with the chicks was more fun, but I refused to let Stan bully us. The big five quietly watched the show.

"Why don't you and your buddies go cruising instead of bugging us? You're not dressed for the beach and we're just having a good time." I said.

Stan looked at the girls. They looked right through him. He shifted his feet. He didn't know how to respond. My comment gave him a way out. If he had any sense he'd have realized that the girls didn't like his hard guy approach. But as I said, he had no common sense.

Jillian pouted and shook her head. "We don't want to see a big fight Stan. We're just having fun at the beach."

Stan faltered. Things weren't going his way.

"Yea Stan, I said. Instead of cruising, you guys ought to go home and get your cutoffs and boards. The surf's great."

"There're red flags all over. Its no good for surf boards," Stan said.

The confrontation sputtered, I thought that he might back off.

Then Rich with his warped sense of humor said, "Why don't you and Del go home and wax each other's boards. That'd be fun."

16

I took the brunt of Stan's sudden response. He pushed me down on the sand and glared at me. Carlson stepped forward to join him.

***

Herman Harris reminded Joe Carlson of his stepbrothers. They could do no wrong according to Loretta, his stepmother. He hated them. Loretta once told Joe that she inherited him from the Colonel's first wife, a drunk. He knew that the Colonel related to all his kids in an authoritative manner. Still, Joe used to try to impress his old man. A few years ago, he gave up. Harris always seemed to do the right thing. He studied hard, doing all the square things, but somehow everyone looked on him as cool. Joe believed he could take Harris. He almost fought him last year when Harris was just a freshman. Joe cared enough about his reputation then not to pick on a freshman. Now he didn't give a shit. Joe touched the knife in his pocket. He wanted to kick Harris's ass for no other reason but that he was popular.

***

"Let me take this asshole."

"No, I'll pound him," Stan said.

The Idiot forgot that Rich had muttered the inflaming words. Sprawled on my back in the sand, I remembered my old man's advice when I was a little kid in Norfolk. *If another kid picks on you and he's bigger, hit him first and hit him right on the nose. That'll hurt him. Then just keep slugging him. Don't fight fair. Kick him in the nuts; thumb his eyes, whatever it takes until he gives up.* Pop had a tough life growing up. He enlisted as a way to get out of the Brooklyn slums in the early thirties. He knew how to fight.

I rose to a squatting position.

I heard Jillian say, "Knock it off Stan. Don't be a jerk."

I stood up and shot out my right fist, hitting Stan right on the tip of his nose. It was enough. I heard the snap. Blood shot out; he grabbed at his nose and bent down. I stepped back and kicked him in the face. Then I grabbed him, moaning and bent over, and ran him into the water. I threw his ass down in the foam. That got all his hard guy clothes dripping wet including the leather huaraches. Bitch'n, I hoped that I ruined the sandals. Let him explain that to his mom.

Carlson headed toward me. I steeled myself for a kicking, hair pulling, kneeing and biting all-out fight.

***

Joe closed on the two fighters, his adrenaline rising with his anger. He wanted to pound Harris. His anger seemed to well up from nowhere these days, overwhelming him. He didn't care who or why he just wanted to tear someone apart. He tossed his cigarette into the water. He saw the lifeguards approach. Joe wanted to fight them. The image of his old man's wrath stopped him. He didn't want a beating from that old Marine bastard.

***

"Hey no fighting on the beach," one of the lifeguards shouted. "We can arrest you both for fighting."

Good, the lifeguards had shut Carlson down. Stan was a blowhard, but Carlson, was dangerous.

"I have to head home now," I said. "This guy started it."

Stan leaned his hands on his knees and spit salt water and blood.

"You better go home and have you mother look at that nose," the lifeguard said to Stan.

I smiled. That infuriated him. Go home and have your mother look at that nose, the lifeguard said. Everyone heard it. Stan stood there speechless holding his nose.

Already a little sunburned, I decided to head home. I knew from experience that I didn't want to spend a week hobbling around in pain with a bunch of blisters. After which, I'd spend a week scratching the itchy, flaking skin. That would cramp my style. I had to fix my motor bike anyway.

I left them standing there at the edge of the foam, grabbed my go-aheads and headed home. I waved at the guys. They gave me the thumbs up sign. The girls acted cool, pretending to ignore the whole thing. I knew that they'd giggle about it later.

3

I heard Jillian as I crossed Orange Avenue.

"Wait Herman."

She strode quickly in her go-aheads, a light white cover-up failing to hide her wiggling breasts in her tight blue swimsuit. Her outspoken manner actually made people like her. She mouthed off to teachers and fellow students alike, but that mouth contained strong white teeth and full lips, which often formed a smile. She was attractive in an overpowering way.

The small town of Coronado allowed few secrets. Her dad was a full Captain and a drunk. The Navy assigned him to some job or another where he couldn't get into trouble until he could retire. Jillian liked to antagonize her long-suffering mother whose claims to aristocracy paled through the years as her husband's camaraderie drinking grew to an addiction to alcohol. Jillian brought home the hoods of the school. As if this navy town's high school could be said to have real hoods. Even the black leather jacket types with motorcycles turned out to be officer's kids with too much money and too much time on their hands.

"Cool the way you handled Stan," she said, grinning. "I live on Glorietta Boulevard. Let me walk with you."
"I didn't wanna fight Huffman. He's such an ass," I said.

"Oh, we all know that. Maybe someday he'll grow up. I don't think Joe will. Stan's his last friend in school as far as I know. He's a little crazy, I think. I had a date with him once when we were both freshmen. He was nicer, and cleaner then. I turned him down for a second date. He acted a little too weird. Sometimes in class, he would make a sound, then turn around embarrassed, I guess to see if anyone noticed."

"Sound?"

"Like he was talking to someone. I think he daydreamed. We all do that, but he existed in a different world."

She tossed her head and smiled directly at me.

"Do you live in the enlisted housing area, Herman?"

"Yea, Dad's a Chief Machinist Mate. He enlisted in 1932 during the depression. He and Mom plan to buy a house when he retires. He wants to get a teaching credential and maybe teach vocational courses somewhere in San Diego, in a couple of years."

"You sound proud of your father."

"Yea, how about you Jillian, are you proud of your father?"

"Call me Jill."

"Dad had it a little easier. He comes from the Virginia Hankins family. His line goes way back, so his family is sort of uppity. They have lots of political contacts. He got an appointment to Annapolis. He did a lot of different stuff in the Navy, but now he drinks too much. He's at sea now as Chief of Staff for some Admiral. At least he can't drink aboard ship."

Jill giggled. "Your hand looks raw, Hermie. You skinned it on Stan's nose. Stop at my house, I'll put a bandage on it or something. My mom's off at some wives club meeting."

She touched me as she said it.

What could I say, of course, I agreed - my lucky day. Our pace slowed as we talked. She bumped against me as we walked. Her legs were strong and shapely, her waist trim, and her smile open and genuine. She chatted incessantly forcing me to look toward her. She was oblivious of the effect of the nearness of her breasts to my concentration. Her swimsuit moved independently of them as she walked, exposing her tan line. My mind drifted from the fight. Finally, she got to her point.

"Do you go to all the beach parties?"

"Most of them," I said. "There's one tonight."

Beach parties happened about every weekend. The kids all spread the word and just showed up. Many brought beer if they could get it. Others just hung out. Usually there was a big bonfire, music from a portable radio, and lots of making out. The parties started at dark and ran until everyone went home or the beach patrol broke it up. When they showed up everybody took off. The beach patrol in this closed community chased people, but never seemed to catch anyone. They were content to break things up. They usually didn't show up unless things got loud.

"I've only been to a couple. My mom forbids me go to them, so I sneak out when I can."

I stopped and grinned at her. "You sneak out. I don't picture you doing that."

"If you knew me better, you could. I wanna go tonight. It's the last one of the summer. I hear it'll be a blast. Why don't you take me?"

Bitch'n, this senior chick asked me to take her to the beach party.

Before I got too excited she hurriedly said, "I know guys don't take dates to beach parties, but it's the only way I can get out. My mom lets me go on dates, but not to beach parties."

"I could get Stan or one of those guys to take me, but they're disgusting."

"Disgusting, huh."

"Yea, did you hear what Stan spread all over the school about Liz? He said she was a baby because she wouldn't pet. Why should he expect her to do anything but neck?"

"Well, aw..."

"Anyway, he has bad breath and he's fat. He was lucky she even went out with him in the first place. Boys that talk about their dates infuriate me. He still hangs out with that Joe Carlson. That's a turnoff for any girl. Why date a druggie? There's no future in that."

As she laid into him, all I could say was, "yea."

"I guess I could get one of the other seniors to take me, but I want to go off to college without a boyfriend. I don't want to start up something right now," she said.

"Huh, well..."

As she went on, I looked at her pretty mouth and glanced down now and then at her cleavage and her legs...those thighs.

"The only thing to do is to go with a guy who wouldn't want to be my boyfriend. You're a sophomore, but you're cool. I don't think you want to get serious."

"Huh, yea." I said.

She finally let me finish a thought.

"So I thought you might take me. I really like the way you handled Stan. He deserved it. I hope he goes to the party tonight and sees us. That would put him in his place."

Nodding encouragement, I took in her whole body, especially the way her tanned thighs disappeared into the tight fitting bottom of her bathing suit. A little red line on her left inner thigh marked the beginning of milky white skin where the suit had slipped upward a bit.

"You'll have to say we're going to a movie if Mom asks."

"Huh, well..." I said as I stumbled on a rise in the sidewalk.

She took my hand firmly in hers, stopping to emphasize her point. I looked into her eyes and saw them soften,

24

then just as quick, turn firm. She continued on, turning slightly to hold my face in her gaze, holding my hand in both of hers. I wondered if Jill intended to control our date so she could drink a little and flirt with the older guys, maybe just use me to get out of the house. Instead of enjoying the party and possibly hitting on some sophomore chick out for a good time, with her I'd be like a dog on a leash. I was thinking along those lines when we got there.

"Come in, my mom's not home," she said.

That got my attention again. My mind bounced around images of her milky white thighs, full boobs and white teeth as she told me about her parents' rules. She couldn't hang out with anyone that wasn't from a senior officer's family or one of the rich families on the island. So why me, I thought as I followed her in. The inside of her place wasn't that much bigger than my folk's duplex, but its picture window looked out at a lawn. My folk's picture window looked out at a parking lot. Our worn carpet covered the whole floor; her family's oriental carpet accented a hardwood floor. The furniture looked new. The couch didn't sag in places like ours. Like my mom, her mom kept the place clean and neat. She sat me down next to her in a little love seat, ignoring the full size couch. She took my hand and examined it as if she knew something about nursing or something.

"There's some ointment I can put on it. I'll go get it," she said.

I sat there looking at how the other half lived. A fireplace and a wooden mantel made up most of one wall. Stained wood molding along the wall-to-wall royal blue carpeting and ceiling edges highlighted the pure white walls. White furniture with royal-blue designs on the fabric added to the wealthy look. Jill's family wasn't rich but they sure did better than my family. I watched the clock on the mantel. Its ticking made me wonder what Jill was doing. What would I say if her mom suddenly walked in?

Then Jill popped into the room from the hall. She had taken off her swimsuit. She wore a terrycloth robe and carried a tube of ointment. Her bare feet highlighted her calves which lead up to those thighs...I pictured her legs and her body under the robe. Stretching her legs out, she wiggled her toes in the thick carpet.

"I had to get out of that suit. It gets so scratchy with all that sand."

She took my hand and gently spread ointment on it. Part of her breast showed when she bent close. Her breasts jiggled unrestrained beneath the terrycloth. Bitch'n.

"Take off your sweat shirt so I won't get ointment all over it." She whispered.

I did. That put only her terrycloth robe between my bare chest and her lush tits. She rubbed the ointment into my hand very gently, leaning on my chest to do it. Some wisps of her sun bleached dark blond hair tickled my nose. I felt her warm softness against my bare chest. Trying to figure out if I could start kissing her right there on the love seat, I put one hand on her back as she rubbed in the ointment. She didn't object. I didn't feel a bra strap. I moved my hand up to her neck. This was a senior girl, my mind was telling me. Did she realize how she was affecting me? But my body didn't have to think, it just

26

reacted. I rubbed her neck and touched her cheek to turn her head toward me.

She turned suddenly. Before I could kiss her, she murmured, "Those cutoffs must be full of sand. Why don't you take a shower here?"

"With you?" just blurted out of me – stupid.

She giggled and pressed against me, watching for my reaction with lidded eyes.

"I hadn't thought of that." She said. "I never showered with a sophomore before."

She turned and peaked out the window as if her mom was due home.

"Let's do it," I said, thinking it's worth a try even if her mom might be home any minute.

She took my hand and pulled me out of the loveseat as if to lead me to the shower.

Then frowning impishly, she said, "Here's Mom now."

A yellow 1959 Oldsmobile 98 pulled into the short driveway. I sighed and pulled on my sweatshirt.

Jill squeezed my hand. "Now remember, we're going to the movies, I think Ben-Hur is playing."

An important looking woman strode up to the door and opened it with a superior manner. She looked down at me, her head held high and cocked to the side.

"Do I know this young man?" She said.

Jill's mom projected confidence, her figure firm, like an athlete's. Not bad legs either. Her white skirt with matching jacket fit impeccably. Standing there in her high heel shoes, she looked like a woman used to getting her way. I could see where Jill got her genes.

"Oh this is Herman Harris, from school," Jill said. "He hurt his hand body surfing so I got him some ointment. We're gonna go to the movies tonight, if you don't have anything planned for me."

She gave Jill a once over look and raised her eyebrow. The brief pause made the room electric. That look said everything. Jill's mom didn't like her daughter wearing only a bathrobe.

"I'm Mrs. Hankins," she said to me extending a hand.

I shook her hand formally. "How do you do, Mrs. Hankins."

"His father's a Commander, mother." Jill said. Another lie.

Mrs. Hankins' expression softened. "I guess that's okay. I must say he looks more clean-cut than some of the unkempt creatures you've brought home, Jillian."

"I'll pick you up at seven, Jill," I said.

I bugged out before Mrs. Hankins could pose any more questions and before Jill could concoct any more lies.

A. J. Converse

4

The walk home took 15 minutes. I heard a neighbor in the duplex screaming at her husband. Boswain Mate Second Class Deacon Morris was in trouble with his wife again. From the sound of it, he chose watching the Padre Baseball game on TV instead of mowing the little patch of lawn in front of their unit. "Deak" as he preferred to be called, liked sports and beer in that order. His showed an easygoing patience with his wife and treated their two boys well. The screaming stopped, probably because he kidded her or something. Soon enough he would be outside, happily mowing the lawn, his wife placated. The kids attended the first or second grade or something. Little brown bundles of energy, they were always getting into trouble. Pop called them the *Katzenjammer Kids*.

Like the Morris', good solid people lived in the housing project. The Navy provided the housing to families of enlisted men on a seniority basis. A petty officer headed most of the families. The units tended to be rundown, housing as they did a series of short-term residents. A screen door swung on a single hinge a few doors down from us. Little kids often ran around the yards in their diapers. The white paint on the units showed wear, peeling off in places and stained with mold in others. The navy tended to neglect their maintenance, something the city fathers criticized.

Chief Petty Officers, Warrant Officers and junior commissioned officers with families lived in homes elsewhere in the San Diego area. Mostly only Lieutenant Commanders and above could afford Coronado homes. Thus, an upper class/lower class thing, with children of

29

senior officers mingling with the kids like me from enlisted men's housing existed in town. Some mingled freely, like my friends, but some were more conscious of class in their selection of friends.

I opened the front door and found Pop watching the Padres on TV. A Chief with over twenty years of service, Pop's head revealed a small but growing bald spot. Like my grandfather's bald spot, it would eventually grow to cover the top of his head. I had the same color hair as he, so I figured I'd be bald when I got older. Pop had an athletic build, which I also inherited, and a big nose, which I had not. He came from sturdy English stock as Mom often said. He and Mom were saving to buy a house after his retirement, so he took advantage of the free Navy housing.

The Padres were playing the Portland Beavers, another oh-hum team in the Pacific Coast League. I don't know why he watched the Padre games. Even major league ball games bored me – too slow. Might as well watch golf on TV, I thought. Pop grew up in Brooklyn watching the Dodgers, who provided heroes for every kid. Baseball was in his blood. A bag of pretzels balanced the rabbit ears at just the right place on the top of the set. They helped to stabilize the picture, which fuzzed up now and then, or so pop said. Mom didn't like him snacking while watching TV. She thought he needed to watch his weight now that he was over forty, but Pop wasn't over weight. His active job kept him trim.

It was Mom who was slightly overweight, a matter to which I never alluded in her presence. She tended to impute into others little flaws that she herself possessed. She'd take offense if anyone dare insult her by pointing out the very same flaw. Mom was a good egg but sometimes I had to tiptoe around her moods and foibles. You can never figure out women, so don't even try, Pop often said.

"What's the haps," Pop said mimicking the current slang the kids used at school.

"You're so cool Pop," I said.

Pop put his thumbs under his belt and grinned. He liked to razz my brother and me. My brother, a junior at San Diego State, had moved to a small apartment with a couple of other guys. Now Pop had only me to tease.

"Staying out of trouble, chasing the chicks on the beach instead of drinking beer," he said.

"I got in a fight at the beach with a senior, but I kicked his ass."

"Don't use that word around here bub," Mom shouted from the kitchen.

She scurried out of the kitchen with a frown. Her pretty Irish face began to flush. The redness seemed to come up her neck to her face in a wave. The blush actuated her freckles and a perky nose. I had to smile at her. She had a quick, chirpy way of talking that was entertaining when she was bantering with Pop; it became grating when she nagged me.

"Sorry, Mom."

"I thought that stuff stopped after junior high school," she chirped, only half-angry.

She put her hands on her hips.

"You look healthy enough; it must have been a short fight."

"He started it. I just defended myself. Remember Pop, what you told me when we lived in Norfolk. You said hit him first and hit him on the nose. That will take the fight out of a bigger kid. That's what I did. It was a short fight. The kid is the son of a Captain and thinks he is hot shit, a real rough, tough, creampuff."

Mom frowned and wagged her finger at me.

Pop smiled a bit and said, "Was he bigger than you?"

"Yep, he's the full-back on the football team." I said.

Pop leaned back and smiled broadly.

"What's that stuff on your hand?" Mom asked. She frowned.

"Oh one of the girls at the beach had some ointment she put on it. I hurt it on Stan's nose. It's swollen a bit. Now I have a date with her tonight. We are going to that beach party I told you about Pop." I said.

I rarely deceived my parents. They were fairly cool, but they insisted on knowing the truth about my activities.

"I don't know about those parties. Things can happen. I don't want you to get some girl pregnant like your cousin Norm did. The girls these days just don't get the moral training they did in my day," Mom said

"Oh Mabel let him be a kid. And if you'd had those high standards that you speak of we wouldn't have fooled around before we got married. As I remember it, we fooled around quite a bit. He won't do anything stupid. Anyway, as soon as one of those parties gets out of hand the beach patrol breaks it up," Pop said. He chuckled.

Only Pop called Mom Mabel. Her name is really Mary, Mary Prudence O'Halloran. She fell for Pop in his sailor suit in the spring of 1940 and they've been together ever since.

Mom smiled and started chirping, "Your charm swept me off my feet against my upbringing Mr. Harris."

"That beach patrol breaks up parties nearly every weekend, Harry. I read about them in the Coronado Journal. They never seem to stop them at the start and they never seem to catch anyone when they break them up. The paper always says everyone scattered and the participants are believed to be college students."

"That's the beauty of living in an isolated Navy town. The public officials don't want to stir up any ill will with the Navy brass by arresting some Admiral's kid." Pop said.

"Well I've gotta go fix that flat on my motor bike." I said before Mom could start sputtering about the beach party thing again.

I changed into some old faded Levis that I wouldn't be caught dead in at school. They worked great for stuff like fixing my motor bike. It didn't take long to get the front wheel off and water test it. I used my old bicycle tube repair kit to glue a small piece of rubber over the hole. When I finished, I decided to run it over to the gas station a few blocks away and get some gas for its tiny tank. That would cost fifteen cents. Gas prices were high now; about 23 cents a gallon, the motor bike went a couple of weeks on a tank of gas.

When I pulled up to the gas pump, I noticed Joe Carlson by the front door of the station buying cigarettes from the machine. Stan and his buddies must have dropped him off. As usual, he looked like he wanted to pick a fight with someone, anyone. Then I noticed a dark car pull up and he climbed in. Three hard looking Mexican guys sat in the car. They weren't townies, probably his drugged out buddies from Imperial Beach. They all wore shades. Carlson didn't notice me and I didn't want him to. The car pulled out with squealing tires. The jerks tried to look tough by laying rubber. There were some navy families in that town at the other end of the Silver Strand from Coronado, but these guys weren't navy brats.

Mom had tacos for dinner. I liked the way she made them, extra greasy, with onions, tomatoes and hot sauce.

After dinner, I called Rich and told him not to pick me up. I'd meet him and the guys at the beach with Jill. Rich's quiet but confident manner combined with a dry sense of humor. His sly smile usually preceded his wry comments. Rich's old man worked for the city in the mayor's office – city development or something. Mr. Levesque was also a big shot in the local VFW.

34

A. J. Converse

Rich owned a used 1949 Plymouth that functioned as the guys' transportation. He acted like an old lady with it. He didn't like getting all greasy playing with its innards, but he spent hours waxing and polishing it. He kept the inside impeccable. We respected his rigidity. If we smoked we cleaned out the ashtray after each ride. We were careful not to spill beer while riding in it. Trash got the heave-oh if there was a trash can around or not. The city streets were better places for trash than inside Rich's car. You could walk anywhere in Coronado but cruising was cool. We all chipped in for gas and drove down Orange Avenue like big-assed birds playing Rock'n Roll loud on the radio.

My date with Jill surprised Rich.

"So what kind of unnatural act did you promise to perform to get her to go out with you?" He said.

I could picture his smile. He knew my folks were probably in the room so I couldn't answer him directly.

"I'm just so cool Rich, she asked me on her own. She followed me home from the beach. I guess I impressed her with the way I handled Stan." I said. But Jill had surprised me too.

"Bitch'n," Rich said.

Mom and Pop sat there trying to look disinterested as I hung up the phone.

5

I got to her house at seven, wearing a striped shirt over my Levies. My car coat topped off my hep look. The only thing cooler than a car coat, was a letterman's jacket. I hoped to earn one this year. I rang the doorbell. Jill popped out immediately, avoiding any last minute quizzing from her mom.

"Let's go," she said.

She grabbed my hand to pull me along for the short walk to the beach. She wore short shorts, an Annapolis sweatshirt and little white tennis shoes. Her breasts didn't jiggle as much as they had in the terrycloth robe that afternoon. *Must be wearing a bra.* I hoped that I could change that later in the evening. Her legs looked like they would get cold. I hoped that I could help with that too.

"We'll be meeting my friends at the party. Will sitting with a bunch of sophomores bug you?" I asked.

"No, it's cool."

She held my arm with both hands and looked up with a grin, as she hustled me along. I could feel her soft tits against me. She bounced along, eager to get to the party. The guys lounged on the sand waiting for us. I guess they were curious about my senior "big five" date. They refrained from spewing forth the typical wise cracks as Jill and I sat down comfortably next to them, a good spot next to the fire. The crowd was growing. Some kids were already drinking. Groups of girls flirted with groups of guys. Later most would pair off, to make out. Someone had a portable radio that was playing *The Battle of New Orleans*. It promised to be a Bitch'n evening.

"Okay, Mo's here. Let's go get a tap," Hampton said.

"Oh that'll be fun, let's do it." Jill said. She stood up bouncing up and down on her tiptoes.

"Let's stay here Jill. The guys will get our beer. Right guys," I said. I hoped to stay at the party with her while my friends got the beer.

"Come on Mo even Larson's going for the tap. You can't be square, come with us. Jill wants to go." Rich said.

Jon gave me a look that said you had better go or I'll razz you the rest of the night. In a couple minutes, I found myself sharing the back seat with Jon and Larson, Jill sitting on my lap. Hampton sat in front, riding shotgun. Rich shifted into gear and let out the clutch smoothly - no burning rubber for Rich.

Jill turned her head and kissed me passionately with an open mouth.

Then she said to the group, "How do you get a tap?"

Hampton said, "We pick up a sailor walking to town from the Amphibious Base. That's the easiest way."

Hampton wore his dark brown hair slicked back on the sides into a duck-ass and cut short on top. His old man was a Captain, but Hampton wasn't much into the class thing. He had something in a cup, probably pilfered it out of his father's liquor cabinet. Hampton got good grades easily with little studying. Teachers liked his shy and polite manner in class. When he got into liquor on weekends, he changed. He seemed to need booze to be sociable. With the guys, he often invented unusual and long swear words. He liked to toss the football or baseball but avoided playing on the school teams. He mostly liked to party, get drunk and chase drunken girls. At the parties, we frequented there were a fair number of drunken girls. By informal consensus, he generally dealt with the sailors, which we targeted as "taps."

"Why don't you just pick up sailors walking out of the North Island Gate?" Jill said.

North Island makes up about two thirds of the whole "island" of Coronado. Actually, Coronado is a peninsula with a narrow strip of sand called the Silver Strand, which connects it to the mainland via a long road that goes south to Imperial Beach. There's a ferryboat service for cars and pedestrians from San Diego directly across the bay. The long drive around the bay keeps it isolated like the island it had once been. North Island is the Naval Airbase. The Amphibious Base is located just south of the village, along the Silver Strand. That's where the Navy trains its frogmen and practices Marine landings.

"Na, those sailors know they don't have a long walk to catch the ferry to San Diego so they usually don't accept rides. The Amphibious base sailors are leery when we stop them, but they know we'll save them a long walk to the ferry landing, so they're a lot easier to pick up." Hampton said.

Coronado had liquor stores, but no real sailor bars, like the ones that proliferated across the bay. Young single sailors wanting to be wooed, screwed and tattooed headed to San Diego. The ten-cent fare fit their budgets and the ferries ran all night.

We headed south, out of town a couple of miles, to the turn for the amphibious base. We made a U-turn there and headed toward the village. We passed by a couple of young sailors that were only seaman. We searched for a Third Class Petty Officer, more likely to be over twenty-one, but not so old as to be wise enough not to mess with a bunch of teenagers. If he appeared alone, it was so much the better. The first time around, we didn't see any promising taps. We continued back to town, made another U-turn and headed back. Many sailors walked the couple of miles to the ferry landing in town for the trip to San Diego at this time in the early evening.

Then we saw him, tall and lanky, walking alone with the collar of his pea coat turned up against the early evening land breeze from the San Diego mainland. The crow on his shoulder and the single red reenlistment stripe lower on his sleeve meant that he was probably over twenty-one. He was white. We wouldn't ask a Negro sailor. Most Negro sailors would probably run from us anyway. Rich pulled the car over to the side of the road just ahead of him. Hampton rolled down the window.

"Hey buddy, if we give you a ride will you do us a favor?" He said.

The sailor looked a bit scared when he saw the crowd. His Adam's apple protruded from his skinny neck. When he saw Jill sitting on my lap, he seemed to relax a bit.

BITCH'N

"What do ya want me to do?" he said with a Midwestern twang.

Hampton acted upbeat and friendly.

"We want ya to get us some beer, we'll buy, and throw in a six-pack for you," he said.

"Okay, I could use a ride."

The sailor climbed in next to Hampton. We decided to get two cases of Budweiser and give the sailor a six-pack from one of the cases. We figured 42 cans of beer should be enough for the five guys plus Jill. Hampton would probably drink two six packs himself and Jon liked beer. Myself, I figured two cans. I really didn't like the stuff. Maybe Jill would have enough to get high and really give me a good time making out. I kissed her. Flushed with excitement she responded, opening her mouth again. I filled it with my tongue. She moved and pressed close. She thought it dangerous to get a tap in Coronado. That seemed to turn her on. Maybe I wouldn't even have to get her drunk. Bitch'n.

We stopped on Second Street, near the corner of Orange Avenue, keeping the engine running. Jill stopped the kissing to watch anxiously. She kept her cheek touching my cheek. My hand slipped to cup her ass. This waiting part always made me nervous. I pictured the sailor coming out with a cop who would then arrest us for underage drinking or something. Jill started wiggling on my lap. Squeezed in the back seat with her weight on me, her squirming aroused another feeling in me that extended in a manner she must have felt. I endured the discomfort and enjoyed the pleasure. She didn't move my

40

hand. She kissed me instead. We were communicating without sound, our bodies and tongues saying something words could not. My mental picture of the cop disappeared.

Too soon, the sailor came out with two cases of Bud. Hampton split out a six-pack for him. Rich dropped the grinning sailor, beer in hand, a couple blocks away, at the ferry landing.

Jon and Hampton opened their beers while Larson examined his can and looked furtively out the window. One night we had picked up a tap and everyone gave him an order. Larson didn't order any beer. He ordered a cigar, not cool at all. It certainly made the sailor feel less intimidated. He actually laughed. The situation made us all look stupid, not like cool cats, but stupid. We sometimes discussed shutting Larson out of the group. But as Jon said, it was fun to tease his sister. Anyway, he was an old friend.

I started a beer and shared it with Jill who cuddled close. Rich cruised to the beach, a ride of about five minutes up 3rd Street to G Avenue then up G to the beach. He parked near a stairway down to the sand. We clambered out of the car. Jill's excited wiggling and kissing affected me in a prominent way. I had to hunch over to adjust things as a knowing Jill stood casually in front of me with the can of beer. She looked sideways at me and asked, "Everything straightened out." I nodded my belt and a loose car coat disguising my situation. Then we walked down to the sand, me feeling especially cool with this sophisticated senior chick.

6

The guys wore car coats or letter jackets, go-aheads or huaraches. The girls wore shorts sweat shirts, and go-aheads. Couples making out, kids drinking beer, they all crowded around a large bonfire. A portable radio played *Lonely Boy*. Rich and Hampton lugged one case and Larson and Jon carried the other three six-packs. Jill and I strolled between them sharing the single beer. I saw Stan and Del, along with their other two buddies, Bobby Champ and Jim Nelson lounging on the other side of the fire. They sipped beers and tried to look tough with their huaraches and letter jackets.

Jon nudged me and said, "Mo look, the four school hoods. Let's go over there and pick a fight."

Jon a husky Pollock lived with his brother and sister and widowed mother a few blocks away from my house. His neighborhood was as expensive as the Country Club area where all the Navy Captains lived. It was close to the bay. His mom inherited wealth. An active member of the hospital auxiliary, she was well known in the village. Jon's blond hair was long and unruly most times. He claimed that his grandfather had changed the family name from some unpronounceable Polish name when he immigrated to the U.S. He instigated many of our escapades. When Rich first got his car, he suggested that we get sailors to buy us beer. The amphibious base circuit was one Coronado High School kids had used for years before we came along but Jon steered us into the practice.

Jill squeezed my arm and said. "You'd better not."

As we settled down near the fire, the radio throbbed with *Turn Me Loose*. A couple of freshman boys dared each other to go in skinny-dipping. Several freshman girls laughed and egged them on. Then amid cheers, one of the boys jumped up and ran for the water. Near the water, and about thirty yards away from the fire, he stripped off his clothes and ran into the surf. All that could be seen were his bare buttocks in the moonlight. Cheers went up from the crowd. A couple of the girls went sneaking toward his clothes to hide them. He noticed them first and came charging out. They squealed and ran back to the fire. Finally, he dressed and came back. Still dripping wet, he plopped down in the sand.

"He's gonna regret that tonight. That sand will work in under his clothes and bother all his body parts. I bet he heads home within an hour. He's a dumb shit." Hampton said.

One of the girls jumped on the freshman, pinning him in the sand and kissing him. That had apparently been the bet. Now covered in sand, he tried to brush it off, but it was impossible. It stuck to his wet clothes.

Someone said, "Hey why don't you go back into the water and wash that stuff off."

The kid said *fuck you* to everyone in general and walked off toward the road.

"What he'll need tonight is a good douche bag," Hampton said.

High, he became talkative and creative, but when he got smashed, he became sarcastic and abusive. We started

43

cutting off his booze if we could, before he hit the smashed stage. He had now downed three beers, putting him at his creative best.

Jill just looked at him. She scrunched closer to me. I could feel the beer and Jill. Both made me warm. Someone started singing *Ninety-nine Bottles of Beer on the Wall*. Someone else shook up a beer can and sprayed him, to shut him up. Everyone laughed.

"At least pick a cool drinking song," Hampton said.

Rich said, "How about that song of yours, Hampton?"

So Hampton sang, "Hey ladi, ladi, ladi, hey ladi, ladi, lo. Drag my balls across the halls; I'm one of the sporting crew."

He started on the second verse when Jill jiggled her beer can and sprayed him. Laughing, she peaked around me and said, "Don't you wish Hampton."

Some of the chicks stripped down to bikinis and put on a show by dancing to music of the portable radio. Hampton gingerly placed his beer can on the sand, stripped to his waist, got up, and danced with them. As the party picked up, a late model Cadillac parked on Ocean Boulevard. A stoned Joe Carlson climbed out with two Mexicans. They escorted him down the steps and along the sand toward the party.

***

Joe's head spun dizzily as his amigos helped him stand. He'd directed them here to sell weed. Now he just wanted to crash. Too much weed, too much booze put him in no shape to stand up or act the hard-ass. At least the voice in his head was gone. His mind drifted, reeling. He forced himself to stay conscious, steadying himself as if balancing on a surfboard. Not friends, the Mexicans just used him to sell pot. Only Stan, a loyal friend since grade school, stuck with him. Classmates avoided him. Now he was trying to get Stan and his buddies hooked. Crap what a life, he thought - My parents don't give a rat's ass what I do, what the fuck...

***

Carlson came stumbling to the edge of the party supported by two Mexicans. He wore scuzzy old unwashed Levis and shades. He looked like the Mexicans found him and picked him up off his ass in some gutter somewhere. I understood at some gut level, his threat to me. A knot of fear tightened in my gut. I knew that dope controlled his life. In 1959 Coronado, cool cats all drank beer. Only scum and criminal types took drugs. Most of the pseudo-hoods here would go on to college, some to the Naval Academy. They would grow up eventually. Not Carlson, he was headed for big trouble. His old man was a Colonel in the Marines, but Carlson, I figured him for jail in the future. Stan for some unknown reason, stayed loyal to him. I guess it was loyalty anyway. Stan was too naïve to see the danger in Carlson's friendship. Most of the pseudo hard guys like Stan, never fought. They just relied on intimidation to swagger their way though the high school scene. Rough, tough, cream puffs we called them. Carlson, no cream puff, fought the way I did, all out, kicking, swinging, biting, everything. But I hadn't lost my common sense to drugs. He scared me, because half the time he was drugged out. Unlike the other high school hoods, Carlson really did hang out in Mexico. That's where he got his drugs.

Carlson and the Mexicans approached kids one at a time. I figured it for the typical shakedown. They'd ask for a donation for beer with an implied threat if the kid didn't cough up some cash. I steeled myself for trouble. I intended to hold on to my money. The other guys tensed up. No one wanted to be punched out, but they were damned if they would give those thugs any money. Strange, Stan and company stayed apart from the shakedown crew. Usually, they relished the shakedown. They especially liked to shake down freshmen.

Carlson shuffled up to Jill and me, with a different approach. The hoods were offering, not demanding. Then I saw them, the reefers. That's what Pop called them, the marijuana cigarettes. They looked odd, twisted at each end. Pop told me that he once tried one when he was a young sailor on liberty in Alexandria, Egypt. He said that after two puffs the ground seemed to fall away so that he was looking down at his elongated legs. He never touched the stuff again. My brother told me that college kids were trying it. They called it Mary Jane to be cool.

Carlson selling marijuana - the little hard core of fear in my gut rose, a familiar feeling, the same primitive thing in me that sometimes turned to uncontrolled rage. It energized me when it appeared. Now the feeling shimmered inside me, like it waited in anticipation. I swallowed hard. I didn't want it here, tonight. We didn't need Mary Jane, or whatever crap they called it, here tonight either.

I noticed a couple of kids buy them, light them up, and stand around trying to look cool.

When Carlson got to us, I stood up and told him to take that shit away from me. He wasn't in a fighting mood, in fact, he seemed stoned. He couldn't fight a teddy bear in his condition. Two of the Mexicans supported him as he made the rounds. The other one, who looked quite a bit older, said nothing. I figured none knew English. What the hell was going on here? Jill just stared at them. I smelled smoke from the reefers some of the kids had lit-up. Other kids stood with their six-packs and started to leave. An ugliness developed between many of the guys and the Mexicans. Sometimes these parties had a fight or two but mostly they stayed friendly. Friendliness disappeared with the reefers. Many kids hated the hoods crashing their beach party and they simply didn't like Mexicans. Some of the younger kids, trying to be cool, bought reefers but the hoods just pissed off a lot of the guys.

Stan Huffman and his buddies bought some of the reefers. Carlson sat down with Stan, took a capsule-like pill, lay down, and passed out. The Mexicans sat down with the Huffman crowd and began to drink beer. I noticed that they weren't smoking anything. The other kids relaxed a bit, but the friendly banter died.

"I guess we ought to move, Rich said. "The beach patrol will be here once they get a whiff of that stuff."

"We don't need those hoods taking over the party with reefers," Jon said. The guys grumbled their agreement.

Stan heard them. "You pussies are always afraid of the beach patrol," he said.

Hampton, now drunk said, "Fuck you Stan and all your relatives back to Clarabelle the Clown."

Stan and his crowd stood and moved the few feet over to where we were sitting. Hampton, Jon and Larson all stood up quickly. Rich took his time and I untangled myself from Jill and stood. Jon moved in front of us guys. He planted himself in front of Stan. If anyone was going to fight, Jon was just drunk enough to take on Stan. He stood nearly as tall and had less flab then Stan.

"Now don't start a fight Stan," Jill said. "It'll bring the beach patrol." She stood close to me, holding my arm with both of her hands. I could feel her breasts enveloping my arm. If she was trying to distract me, it was working.

The beach patrol started toward us as soon as they noticed the commotion. I happened to look over toward the road and saw their jeep headed our way.

"Speak of the devil." I was relieved to see the old jeep headed toward us. A big fight with these assholes would ruin the whole deal with Jill. She'd want me to take her home. No, this wasn't what I had in mind for our date at all.

The jeep's headlights danced at crazy angles as the cops drove across the dunes toward the bonfire.

"You better run Stan. They won't look the other way for marijuana," Rich said.

Stan said, "Fuck," and he and his three idiot buddies took off running. The Mexicans got up and ran. Everyone

48

scattered, exploding in all different directions. Some stumbled, drunk, trying to carry their six-packs with them. Others ran like crazy. Several chicks laughed and dashed off with boys. The dancing chicks, still in bikinis, tried to hold on to their other clothes while running - cute. Only Carlson, who was passed out, stayed.

7

I led Jill along the beach near the water, away from the others. We ran about a quarter mile along the water line. Then we turned away from the water and up the beach into some dunes. I carried a full six-pack. She giggled with the effects of the beer and the excitement. It was half-fun, half-scary to run from the beach patrol. We knew we'd have a great story to tell at future beach parties. When I found a comfortable looking spot, we settled down amongst the pickle weed, just in front of the dunes. I opened two new cans and handed her one.

She looked at me under half closed eyelids, "Are you trying to get me drunk, Hermie?" she said.

"Well, yea, actually."

She cuddled close and took a long pull on the can of beer.

"Its working," she said.

We had a couple more beers. The full moon shined through a sliver of clouds. A light land breeze warmed our faces. I kissed her. She rolled on top of me. I untangled myself from the car coat and flung it a few feet away. I felt her body move against me. Would this turn into one of those frustrating nights leaving me to go home with a case of blue balls, I wondered.

After a few minutes, Jill raised her head and whispered, "Lets move back into the dunes some more."

A. J. Converse

We had been lying right where the flat sand, with scattered patches of pickle weed, started to turn into dunes. I shook off the towel and we gingerly walked deep into the dunes and pickle weed. We found a place that Jill liked, well hidden form the road and the beach areas.

Doing it on a towel on the sand can be hazardous, so I put the towel down and spread it out. I guessed she might have had sex once or twice before, probably more experience than me. She lay down, pulling me on top. I knew she was so high she didn't care about me being only a sophomore. The sand didn't deter us. She exuded heat and matched my heaving movements. I felt her sexuality. The excitement of the night, the beer, and running from the beach patrol stoked our mutual desire. The bra came off, the sweatshirt pulled up to her neck. We rolled around on the towel. Her breasts pressed against my chest. Feeling the passion in her eager movements, I slid a hand low between her legs. I felt her touch on me. She moaned and pushed me off.

"Oh god that's good, but stop, we have to stop," She said, breathing her words.

About to burst, I said, "Come on just a little more."

But the moment was over, Jill had recovered her control and the rest is part of the history and legends of beach parties in Coronado. We sat for a while after I calmed a bit, unfulfilled. She had sobered up and sat quietly.

"I'm sorry we can't go further…it was so nice…it was just for tonight." She whispered, almost breathless. I realized it had affected her as much as me. It was more than a little humping with our clothes on.

"You know this doesn't mean anything between us. I picked you because you won't be snowed over me. I don't need that. I'm going away to college next year and I don't want any baggage. I didn't plan to go this far with you. You're a friend. So when I see you at school, I'll say hi. But that's it, no more dates." She said it quickly leaning close.

I swallowed the relief I felt. It turned out to be a dream come true for a sixteen year-old like me - no entanglements, no commitments, just some bare tit, grabbing, and gasping. She couldn't get pregnant from that.

"One thing, Mo, I don't want to hear any details at school," she said.

"I don't kiss and tell. I'll just tell the guys we necked, no details," I said.

I meant it too. Blabbing about a girl, any girl, all over school, would make potential conquests avoid me. They wouldn't want their escapades spread all over school. I sure didn't want to risk being the target of Jill's cutting rhetoric. The best way for a guy like me to succeed with other girls was to keep quiet about our fun on the beach. It had turned out to be a bitch'n night. The only bad part of it was I couldn't tell my buddies I gotten bare tit from one of the big five.

I got her home by midnight and got a big warm kiss at the door.

"Don't forget Hermie," she said, "It's our secret."

The next morning, I woke with guilt born of years of attending church with my mom. What we had done was so real. What did it mean with this girl, Jill. Suddenly she was no longer on a pedestal as one of the big five. Her nose was a bit crooked. Maybe her waist was a bit thick. She wasn't a perfect ideal girl, but just another chick.

8

The morning after my date with Jill, I got up at four. Groggy but awake, I drank a cup of coffee, feeling vaguely guilty. The events of the night before seemed like a dream. I guess too much Sunday school where teachers hammered in the idea that sex equaled sin bothered me. Mom and Pop never said much about sex. We never had that talk. I guess they assumed that I would learn by osmosis or something. Actually, religion inhibited the subject. They probably procrastinated until they realized I had picked up everything anyway. I worried that our kissing with tongues would give me a dreaded kissing disease or something. I knew that wasn't true, but, still...Of course, Mom probably figured that the less I knew the better. She was always preaching about teenage pregnancy.

Finally, more awake, I went outside to retrieve my papers. Damn, just looking at the stacks of Sunday LA Times made me want to crawl back into bed. Resigned, I got the wire cutters out of the toolbox on my motor bike and sat down on our small concrete porch. The distributor had dropped the papers in three stacks of 40 each. Each stack was wrapped tight with a piece of wire. I cut the wires and dully looked at the headlines - nothing important on the front page.

Deak Morris opened his door next to our porch and headed for his car in his dress whites. I saw him sometimes in the early morning when he had drawn the duty on the base. On those occasions, he worked for the Officer of the Day. He was cheerful this morning and gave me a wave. He had confided in me one morning that he liked Sunday duty because it was slow and he and the duty officer generally watched TV all day. He liked the full breakfast, which he got free at the mess hall. He called it good duty.

"Morning Mr. Morris," I said.

"Hey there Harris, working hard huh. What do ya use the money for beer or broads?"

"Both."

"Your old man has trained you right."

Chuckling, he plopped into his old Ford coup.

Pop told me Deak's story once. A lifesaving act got Deak out of working in the laundry on a destroyer, one of the few assignments black sailors ever got in the Navy. It seems that one time as his destroyer steamed off the coast of Korea, two white sailors working in a deep compartment that was poorly ventilated fell unconscious. Morris came out of the laundry compartment and spotted a group of their shipmates standing around waiting for a rescue crew to show up with oxygen masks. Without hesitating, he took a deep breath and climbed down into the compartment. Morris hoisted one on his back, grasped one by the collar, and manhandled them up the narrow ladder to fresh air. The rescue crew later estimated that he had held his breath four minutes while rescuing them. The navy awarded him the Silver Life Saving Medal. Pop said it would have been the gold version if he had been white. Better, for him, the Captain honored Deak's request to transfer to the deck department. Within six months, he took the exam for third class and passed. A year and a half later, he made second-class and now he was shooting for first class.

Pop turned philosophical when he described Mr. Morris' feat. He said the world is full of rules. We all follow them most of the time. We don't walk down the middle of the street. We use the sidewalk. A man doesn't enter an unventilated compartment after shipmates and risk needing rescue himself. He waits for a rescue team. But once in a while we all look into the abyss and realize we can break a rule and take the chance. Mr. Morris instinctively took a chance and he accomplished something considered impossible. The surface of our reality assumes all the rules are followed all the time. But actually, they are followed only part of the time. There is a great fuzziness to the world. The bad are not always punished and the good are not always rewarded. But rules are followed enough to keep civilization together.

The quite stillness of early morning made me think of stuff like that. I noticed that my ass ached already from the hard concrete on the porch. I started inserting the papers in the plastic bags provided by my distributor. The foggy morning air kept the temperature warmer than usual.

By 4:30 a.m., I finished bagging the papers. I loaded up a total of ten papers, five on each side bag and headed out to First Street. By habit, I followed the pattern of streets, up First Street, down Second Street with side trips up B Avenue, up C Avenue etc., then I road straight down Second Street about halfway. Finished with that load and fully awake, I headed home to restock my papers.

That first leg took me about ten minutes. Including the time I spent restocking and riding back to the route, I could do the entire route in three hours on a Sunday. Usually I enjoyed riding the village streets in the still morning air before anyone was up. The smell of salt and the ocean stirred my senses. I didn't dawdle through my routine this time because I wanted to meet the guys at the beach later and I needed extra sleep. Football practice and the paper route built my fatigue during the week, so I caught up my sleep on weekends when I could. I hoped to sleep from 8 am to 11 am. Stories about the party would be circulating among the kids at the beach. I wondered what happened to Joe Carlson the previous night. Did the beach patrol catch anyone else? Did they do anything about the marijuana? The kids on the beach knew the haps. Something about the sale of marijuana in our secluded little world - beer was okay, Mary Jane scared me. Even the name had an ominous ring to it – like a pretty girl that hid a trap under her skirt. They made rope out of it and called it hemp. Why smoke rope? Weird.

Most of my customers on the first half of my route lived in little cottages built in the 1920s and 1930s. Small but expensive, they usually had a detached garage, which opened to the alley that ran between each lettered avenue. Most of the owners were Lieutenants and Lieutenant Commanders or local businessmen. The higher-ranking officers' families and some of the town's elite and their families lived in the newer area in larger houses that had conventional attached garages that opened to a driveway. They were on larger lots. Still they wouldn't be considered anything out of the ordinary in most cities. One customer lived across the street from Joe Carlson. As I rode by, I noticed all the lights on at his house, very early for Sunday. A police car idled in front of the house.

My route ended in Carlson's neighborhood. The owners of the mansions along the beach consisted of rich farmers from the Imperial Valley like Katie Gutierrez's family or other wealthy people who had discovered Coronado as a place for a second home. None of them received the San Diego Union. Most received the Wall Street Journal or something like that by mail. I finished my route about 7:30 am, road the motor bike home, ate some breakfast and hit the sack.

At 11:30, I headed for the beach. I walked past Jill's house with some excitement after the events of the night before, but the house was quiet. She stirred my thoughts - half hoping to find her sitting outside on the porch and half dreading that she would be there. She wasn't.

When I got to Ocean Boulevard, I saw Rich, Jon and Hampton already sprawled on the beach, without Larson. I walked up, tossed off my go-aheads and sat down. "Hi, what's the haps?" I said.

"Larson's old man smelled beer on his breath so he restricted him," Jon said.

"Well fuckin-A he should a taken a mint." Hampton said.

Rich smiled. "What's with you navy brats anyway? A little beer; why is it a big problem? My pop just tells me to stay out of trouble. He doesn't check my breath when I get home."

"Mom trusts me and she's usually asleep when I get home." Jon said.

"Anyone besides Joe Carlson get caught last night?" I said.

"Na, it was the same old deal, the patrol picked up Carlson - they had to. He was out to the world when they got there. I saw it all from the dunes near my car. They carried him to the beach patrol jeep and drove off," Rich said.

"I saw a police car in front of his house this morning while I was doing my paper route. I think he's in trouble," I said.

"They're probably figuring out some way to punish him without actually arresting him. I bet his old man is pissed," Rich said. "I wonder if he knew about the drugs."

"Knowing this town, not only don't they know but they don't want to know. Knowing would explode the dorky civic leaders' image of their precious village. Not cool, oh the scandal," Hampton said.

He lifted his shades and peered out at us. In rare form – he probably hit his old man's liquor cabinet earlier this morning.

"The city fathers don't want a 'rep' like San Francisco where everyone smokes weed and every bar uses topless waitresses."

"Weed?" I said.

"It's what all the beatniks call it."

The guys never asked me what happened with Jill. I guess they just figured we made-out or something. The final analysis of the big last-of-the-summer beach party - it was broken up by drugs first, then the beach patrol. I did get bare tit off a senior and almost...sort of...third base, bitch'n. For the next several weekends, Joe Carlson could be seen polishing police cars at the town's police station. He started his senior year as if nothing happened.

9

At school Monday, I got my locker assignment and stuff in homeroom, then I headed out to my new locker to stash some of the opening day materials. Freshmen wearing beanies filled the halls. Hazing of freshmen began and ended with the beanies, which ended up in trashcans by noon. Everyone knew the freshmen anyway.

I saw Carlson hanging around by the lockers with Stan and his group. They stared at all the chicks and flashed intimidating stares at new freshmen boys. Wearing unwashed Levis, unbuttoned shirts over white t-shirts, and black stained huaraches, they created a little island of menace in the hallway - not cool - jerks.

I met Hampton and started walking along with him.

"What're you gonna do about Stan?" He's just waiting to get back at you," Hampton said.

"I'm gonna meet him eyeball to eyeball to show I'm not intimidated. He's a regular asshole. I'm not afraid of him or that little pussy Del. Carlson is another story. He's dangerous. Stick with me while I stare down Stan, Hampton. Watch Carlson. Make sure he doesn't pull a knife or something." I said.

"Hey, man, I'm a lover not a fighter," but he was right there by my side as we walked up to Stan and his crowd.

I stood directly in front of Stan. "Looks like you hurt your nose." He looked foolish all decked out as a hard guy with a bandage on his nose.

"I can take you any day, Harris." He said.

Carlson coughed, cleared his throat, and said, "You're on my list Harris."

***

Joe felt his body tense and his anger grow. His craving for a cigarette put him in a foul mood. Hooked on cigarettes, hooked on weed, hooked on alcohol and starting on hard drugs, his body actually twitched sometimes. At least he didn't hear that voice. The weed suppressed it. As long as he could smoke the stuff once in a while, he could handle things. And cigarettes, he needed cigarettes all the time now. He wanted this year over so he could leave school and its stupid rules forever. He wanted to drop out at age 16 but his old man said no. Once he turned 18 and got out of school, he intended to leave his bastard father and his bitch of a stepmother forever. Then he could smoke all the dope and cigarettes he wanted.

Harris, Mister hot shit, yea, more like a warmed over turd, son of a navy chief, not a marine colonel like Joe's old man. He wanted to pound Harris' ass. He couldn't explain the primitive hatred he felt. Mo, they called him, something to do with his fighting in junior high school. Joe wanted to fight him some day. Then he would kick Harris's ass.

***

Carlson reeked of cigarettes.

62

"What are you gonna do, knife me in the back? That's your style." I said.

I knew he wouldn't do anything in the hall. The local cops and school officials already had him on a short leash. Hampton stood there stoically but tongue-tied.

"You think you and your buddies can take us," Stan said.

"I don't expect my friends to fight my battles and I don't hide behind them. What you gonna do, have Del help fight me? You sure can't handle me yourself," I said. "Or are you gonna have Carlson pull a knife, and then try to take me?"

"Don't mess with us. Our Mexican friends will carve you a new asshole before they kill you." Carlson said.

That scared me, but I held my face blank.

"Just try that Carlson, you're already half-way to jail. If the cops knew how deep you were into your shit, you would be in jail now. Did your daddy's influence keep you out of jail yesterday?"

Joe cleared his throat. "Fuck you." He said.

"Fuck you." I said. Then Hampton and I walked away.

The view and smell was better ahead in the hall. The big five gathered around Jill's locker wearing tight sweaters, short flared skirts and bobby socks with saddle shoes. Individually adorable with lipstick, perfume and swirling tresses, their combined look and scent created a section of paradise right there in the hall.

Rich and Jon sauntered our way wearing short sleeve shirts, chinos and black loafers with white socks. None of us guys dressed like hoods. We joined Larson as he fumbled with his nearby locker and grinned at the chicks. Jill turned from her locker and chimed in with the other four girls to greet me, "Hi Hermie," as we huddled briefly by Larson's locker, a ritual before our first class.

"Hi Hermie," Rich mocked.

The guys laughed.

I shrugged my shoulders and said, "Can I help it if they're all snowed."

Hampton said, "Un-fucking-mother-of-hairy-balls-christ-believable. What's the secret?"

I shrugged. "I'm a cool cat."

Jon said, "Hey Hampton, you looked a little tense when you and Mo were talking to Stan and those scum bags."

"I'm never tense, man. Taut and primed, that's me. I was covering Mo."

"Way to go. They didn't look scared though."

"Next time you back him up hot shot." Hampton was getting pissed.

"It's cool man," Jon said and cuffed him on the arm grinning. "I'd like to go a few rounds with Stan. I bet I could kick his ass."

The bell rang and we all split up. We planned to meet again for lunch. I headed to geometry class with Jon. We were about the same height and weight in junior high. Now he stood taller, bigger. He didn't have any baby fat like Stan. He was just big.

"So are you gonna tryout for football again this year?" He asked.

"Yea, I did okay last year. I got to play a lot on the JVs, but you know Coach Adamson, he plays favorites." I said.

"Yea, that turd's the reason we don't win very many games. I like to play, so I'm trying out today. Wish we had a better coach. You gonna keep the paper route – and Jill, what about her? He said.

"Jill's history. That was a one-time thing. She just wanted someone to take her to the beach party. She lied to her mom and said my dad is a Commander. I'd be hard for her to keep up that lie if she went out with me again. The date worked out pretty good for me."

He tweaked me on the arm. "Did you plank her? You were going at it in the car."

"Plank her?" I laughed, stopped and turned to face him. "Plank her? Where did you come up with that? You been taking lessons from Hampton? No I didn't plank her, a little French kissing, that's all."

"I sure'd like a shot at one of those big five."

"If you do good in football, they'll think you're a big stud." I said.

"I am a big stud."

"Yea, yea, so which one do you like the most?"

"No question, Liz Edgerton," he said.

"Yea, you and every other guy in school," I said. "Just imagine that naked body in bed."

"Bed, hell I'd be happy just to French kiss her. That would last a lifetime, I think."

I laughed. "Knowing you Jon, I doubt it."

Liz's father, a US Navy Chaplin and a Commander, brought her up a good Christian. That bugged most guys in the school. She was an untouchable beauty to our agony. Her long dark hair complemented her lightly tanned skin. Long legs and a narrow waist complemented her blue eyes and nearly black hair. She didn't mind flirting but drew the line there. All the boys had the hots for her but most chickened out when it came to asking her for a date - the risk being turned down, I guess. She was cherry. I'm sure that she wrote me off as an underclassman and son of an enlisted man, someone she would never consider dating. She did flirt with me sometimes and there was that one dance. She almost dropped her reserve when her body pressed against me. She quickly recovered and wouldn't dance with me again. Someone would get to her someday. She couldn't deny her urges forever.

Football practice went as expected. Coach Bernard Adamson had already selected his first string offensive and defense – all his favorites. At the start, Coach gathered us all around and gave us the talk. No beer drinking, no carousing, stay off the beach. Swimming, he said elongated the muscles and he wanted ours short and compact - for damn sure, he said no smoking. Most of the players broke these rules all the time, but he never really made an effort to check on them.

He chuckled, a deep growl of a chuckle, "Be careful with the girls, don't screw them the day before a game. They'll sap your energy." Then he let out with his notorious laugh, a long low sound, almost forced, that went on and on, making us uneasy. Some of us chuckled and shuffled our feet. Finally, he cut it off and looked around at us.

"Okay, now hustle out there. The assistant coaches are waiting."

The coach strutted around the practice field barking orders, his beer belly belaying his admonishments to get in shape. A commando or something during the war, his current physique reminded me of a walrus, not a commando, but no one argued with him.

Jon hated the coach. He called him Bernie the Bastard or just plain, *that fat shit.* A lot of the players called him that behind his back, but still he scared them. Adamson slapped his players on the side of the helmet, hard, to show his displeasure. Brought up to be respectful of authority figures, I referred to him as Coach. Jon could have been on his favored list because his mom was well known in civic affairs, but his disgust spilled over.

Adamson reacted predictably. Jon was a major recipient of the coach's helmet slaps and blistering comments.

The bastard never chewed out or hit certain players. He favored sons of Navy Captains and Commanders and important people. Not necessarily the best players and in a couple cases, clearly the worst, Adamson favored them because he knew where his bread was buttered. He kissed up to their parents. Del Webber showed up on Adamson's list as first-string defensive end. He didn't have the size or speed for any sport. No athlete, he couldn't get out of his own way, but his old man was a Captain and his best friend Stan was first-string fullback. Not that Stan was any good at fullback either. Slow and lumbering, Stan would have done better as a tackle. My friend Jon stood almost as big and moved a lot quicker off the mark. But Stan wanted to play fullback, so Adamson put him in that position.

Jon and I missed any list. The coach called us scrubs. He didn't rank us, although he said he expected to post a second string list by the time of the first game. He said some of us scrubs would make the second team.

I caught every pass, made every tackle and every block in the first practice. That didn't seem to impress the coach. Jon did as well as me. He outplayed Stan in every regard, but Adamson took pains to berate him for any slight imperfection. He stayed on his ass all the time. After an hour and a half of Adamson's warped version of coaching, he called for wind sprints to end the practice. He lined us up according to position, saying that whoever came in first in the wind sprints in each position would be first string the next day. I ran my ass off and won each group of sprints.

As I left the gym after practice, I noticed Carlson and his two Mexican buddies by the door. They met Stan and his group after practice. Jim Nelson showed up with them at the gym too. He didn't play football but he ran track, the 440. I figured that marijuana would eventually ruin them as athletes.

I noticed Carlson started talking to someone inside the building. I heard the coach's voice, strange - Carlson friendly with the coach?

Sore and achy all over, I headed home from the first practice. I needed to stay awake for an hour at least, to get my homework finished before I could hit the sack. I'd have to get up early for my paper route. Football and the paper route made my life difficult, but girls liked athletes and I liked girls, and I needed the paper route money to chase girls, so there you go. It looked like I'd just have to gut it out.

I planned to study about an hour each night and several hours Saturday and Sunday. That way I'd be able to juggle the schoolwork and football and continue my paper route. I put money away for a car for the same reason I played football - girls.

Pop started to look at some cars for me. He said he'd have to approve any deal I made. He'd decide which car. I let it ride. At least I'd have some wheels. I had a license and drove my parent's car now and then, but rarely in the evening. With my own car, I would be free to cruise, pick up girls and drive myself to school each day - bitch'n.

10

A few days later the coach, true to his word, did post a new list of first and second-string players. Jon caught up with me in the hall after he saw it.

"Hey Mo, did you see the bastard's list? He posted it this morning. That fat shit doesn't know how to pick a team."

Jon's face was red.

"Yea, he plays favorites. He doesn't care about picking the best team. He's such an asshole. All that stuff about winning the wind sprints was pure horseshit." I said.

"That strutting jerk Stan Huffman is first string fullback again this year. I'm way better than him." Jon fumed.

"I know but his old man is a Captain. Of course, it doesn't help your case that the coach knows that you despise him. Take Del, anyone can play better than he can. His old man is a Captain too. Plus, his head is so far up Adamson's ass, it's hard to see how he can breathe. The coach plays favorites."

Jon laughed at the picture of Del walking around behind Adamson. "The coach should have made him water boy, he spends so much time acting as his assistant. You should have been first string on offense and defense, but the coach put him down as first-string defense and that skinny senior as first-string offensive end - at least Del's only first string on defense."

"Yea, that pussy can't play football. He ought to go out for band or something instead. He'd make a great flutist. Can you see him out there at half-time marching with the band with a flute?" I said.

"What about defense? You should have been picked as first-string linebacker, Jon. The coach doesn't have anyone half as good as you on defense."

"He picked that little Mexican kid, Sergio De La Puente. That kid's tough, but he can't hit like me. He's too small."

Jon was being nice to the new kid. Ordinarily, he would have said something like *He's a fuckin' wetback.*

"Yea, I wonder what connection he has." I said.

"I'm about ready to quit and tell the coach to shove the list up his ass." Jon said.

"Yea, but stick it out. You're a good player. Eventually he'll have to play you or look like an idiot. Once we earn our letters this year, we can drop football. You know how the chicks dig lettermen."

The reference to chicks and letters made Jon shift gears.

"Yea, chicks," he answered.

I knew the coach managed to win a few games by playing certain scrubs a lot without recognizing them officially except for their letter sweaters. Chicks went bananas over lettermen, so the letter he gave out satisfied most guys at least for one year. Not a lot played all four years. What's the use? Adamson always played the 'in' kids, not the best players. The school didn't seem to mind that we rarely had a winning season.

Carlson and his two Mexicans met Stan's crowd just about every day after practice. I hoped they'd be caught smoking the stuff and get kicked off the team. That would give me a better chance to play.

Around the end of September, we played our first game - against an Oceanside team. Jon and I sat on the bench as Stan and Del generally screwed up on the field. For the kickoff, Del lined up as a blocker and secondary return runner. The Oceanside players ran right through him. Stan performed a little better. He managed to partially block a rather small player who got in on the tackle anyway. When he carried the ball, he managed to gain only one yard. By the end of the first quarter, we trailed 14 to 0.

Adamson looked around, his face and neck red. He chomped on his unlit cigar. Twisting his short body so that his belly pointed toward the field and his head at me, he waived his clipboard.

"Harris, go in for Webber." He barked.

I ran on the field like a shot before he could change his mind.

"Webber, I'm in for you," I shouted at Del as I took his place as right defensive end.

The play came right at me, a runner behind two blockers, a guard who had pulled, and the full back. I went low and the two blockers went over me stumbling as I hit the

72

runner behind the line. I had backed them up a couple of yards. Then Jon entered the game, replacing Stan. He broke up a fullback draw play and stopped the runner after a one-yard gain.

It went like that for the rest of the game. The coach made substitutions of good players for the starters enough to keep the score respectable. We got one touchdown when Jon deflected a pass to one of our seniors down near Oceanside's goal line. The surprised senior trotted in to the end zone untouched. The final score was 24 to 7.

Jon and I met up with Rich and Hampton for the after game dance in front of the gym across from the football field. A slight breeze blowing toward the ocean kept the evening cool and clear. Larson's restriction kept him home. Stan, Del, Bobby Champ and Jim Nelson stood around outside in their hard guy Levis, letter jackets and huaraches trying to look tough. I went inside and danced with a couple of sophomore chicks. I passed when the guys wanted to go find a tap. There was my paper route in the morning and I was beat. I headed home. I needed the sleep. They split, headed for Rich's car.

As I started home, I spotted Joe Carlson and the two Mexicans talking to Stan and his group. Stan strutted around, acting like he was hot stuff after gaining about 20 yards altogether in the game. What a jerk. I had to walk right by them. I kept my face natural as I approached. I didn't need a confrontation. I was too tired to screw around with their posturing. Sergio De la Puente, the transfer student from Imperial Beach, and an older Mexican man joined the group just then. Stan didn't miss the opportunity.

"Hey Harris," he said, "buy some reefers from me and Joe and I'll forget about beating the crap out of you."

They wanted an excuse to gang up on me.

I looked at Bobby Champ. "Are you really that low, Bobby?" I said.

Then I looked at the Mexican man and said, "Who's this, your supplier?"

Carlson stopped his hacking cough and spit on the grass.

"Shut the fuck up," Carlson said. "That's Mr. De La Puente to you."

Sergio De La Puente said something in Spanish to the older man and the two walked off and climbed into a late model Cadillac. I waived down Rich as he and the guys drove by. Carlson had already moved up close and intimidating. Stan had grabbed my arm. I didn't stand there and wait for Carlson to hit me. I yanked my arm from Stan, rushed over to Rich's car, and hopped in.

"Bug out." I said.

"Holy shit, were you mouthing off to all those assholes?" Jon said.

"Yea, I'm glad you guys came along. How about dropping me at home before you look for a tap - I gotta get up early tomorrow." I said.

Joe Carlson, Stan and their buddies stayed where they were, glaring at us. Jon turned in his seat and gave them the finger.

Rich said, "Shit, now they'll be after us."

After the frustrating game, Jon was up for a fight. "Those turds; I'd like to kick their asses. I say we go back there right now and do it. I'd like a shot at Stan, what a douche bag."

"Count 'em, Jon. There are seven of 'em to five of us and a couple of 'em are Mexicans. Then there's that Mexican man in the Caddy." Rich said.

"I'd still like to pound those assholes," Jon said.

I cuffed him on the shoulder while I said to Rich, "Drop me at home, I'm in no shape for a rumble. They won't come after us. They wanna sell that weed. Those bastards aren't just smoking it, they're pushing. That's why Carlson hangs out with those two Mexicans. They supply it."

"What about that new Mexican kid and the older man, who the hell are they?" Rich said. He was already pulling away, hoping that Jon would cool off.

"That kid's name is Sergio de La Puente," I said. "Carlson said that's his old man. Maybe he was introducing him to some of the other football players. He didn't seem to speak English. I think he might be some sort of big shot in Mexico."

"He should be introducing the old man to you and Jon instead of those assholes, your cooler. Why's that kid get so much playing time? He's not big enough for football," Rich said.

"You know the coach, Rich, he has his reasons. The old man's probably paying him off," I said. I didn't know then how close my guess was to the truth.

They dropped me at home. Pop sat watching Sergeant Bilko on TV. Private Doberman was in some sort of trouble again. Mom came in from the kitchen when she heard me.

"How was the game?" Pop said.

"I got to play and made a couple of good tackles, but we lost the game," I said.

I hit the sack and slept until my alarm went off at 4 am. I spent the weekend doing my paper route and studying.

11

Monday, Larson told us that his parents officially lifted his restriction. We gathered at our lockers and agreed to meet for lunch at the usual spot on the school patio. On my way to my first class, I ran into Jill. She usually just said "hi" to me at school. Now she wanted to talk to me. She smiled.

"Hi Hermie," she said in her best cutesy manner. "I have a favor to ask. Katie Gutierrez needs you to take her to the Sadie Hawkins Day Dance."

Whoa, another of the big five wanted a date... Katie, she was luscious.

As Jill described it, the date with Katie appeared to be another one of those courtesy dates like my date with her. That date with Jill worked out great. How could I pass up a date with Katie, courtesy or not? Anyway, Jill insisted.

"Katie will ask you, if I tell her you said okay. She doesn't want to be embarrassed with you telling her no. She wants to ask you in front of Del. He follows her around trying to get a date with her. At first, she though it was cute, now his big crush bugs her. She means to end his infatuation so he'll stop hounding her. If she asks you to the dance in front of him, he'll get the message. That should bring him down to earth," she said.

A picture of Katie Gutierrez in her maroon bikini flashed in my mind. Her rich dad owned a big farm in El Centro but maintained a mansion in town, at least as near to a mansion as I had ever seen. A shy Mexican, she always referred to herself Spanish. Like with the other big five girls, she generally ignored enlisted men's kids like me. But God, she had a body that just wouldn't stop. Maybe a long shot, but how could I refuse this opportunity? My heart started thumping. This chick made it hard to appear cool.

"Okay, yea, okay, cool," I said. I didn't feel cool. *Holy shit, Katie.*

"Don't you have English with Mrs. Evans at 2:00?" Jill said. "Del and Katie have Chemistry on the other side of the hall at the same time. Stand in front of your room a few minutes before class."

I made it to English class a few minutes before 2:00 and stood out front of the room. Del and Stan walked up the hall. I doubted Stan would take a difficult class like Chemistry. He probably took something easy like Earth Science to get his science credit. Del's Chemistry class happened to be on the way. We exchanged some glares. I put on my best hard guy face. Stan's look was ridiculous. He and Del wore their regular get ups, huaraches and all. I almost laughed. Del wore the same Levis and t-shirt and Mexican sandals as Stan. A brain, Del got good grades. He fell under Stan's influence when Stan's folks moved next door when they attended elementary school. He looked out of place in his hard guy pose. He kept it up to stay part of Stan's group - dorky Del, trying to be hard.

Then, along came Katie for her Chemistry class. She spotted me and smiled. She strolled across the hall right in front of Del, swinging her books in her arms. Del looked like he was about to ask her something. *God, she had a pretty smile.*

"Oh Hermie, will you go to the Sadie Hawkins Day Dance with me?" She said.

"Huh, yea, sure."

Wow, she had asked right out. Tongue-tied, I just stood there. Her white blouse filled with promise and her soft brown skin radiated warmth that I could feel. She held me with her eyes. Her image stuck in my mind, like a photograph of the highest quality. I felt more than saw every detail, from the fine translucent hairs on her arm to her natural thick eyebrows. For only an instant, I stood there transfixed, but it felt like a century. Her scent enveloped me. If she wasn't as good looking as Liz Edgerton, she was a close second. I fumbled, searching for something cool to say.

"Huh, aww..."

"Great," Katie said. "I'll call you about it. Is your number in the book?"

"Yep," I said.

I glanced across the hall. Del's face reddened a bit and Stan gave him the old shrug. Then Stan headed off to his class. Del ducked into Chemistry class, hiding his expression. Katie turned casually, and glided into the Chemistry class. I stood there stupefied. I hoped that she wouldn't have second thoughts when she saw my address in the phone book.

My mind wandered in English class. I thought about Katie's golden skin and soft brown eyes. She had to be the second hottest chick in the school, Liz Edgerton being the hottest. However, I admitted to myself that she might indeed turn out to be number one. I had a date with her and a bird in hand was better than Liz Edgerton in the bush. At that point, Ms. Evans asked me some sort of question. I stammered a simple "huh." Ms. Evans stared at me a minute and turned away and asked someone else. I guess she understood adolescent mental states. I was a good student. I guess that's why she didn't press me. The time flew by and I soon found myself walking toward football practice.

It consisted of the same old stuff. The scrubs held dummies for the first string players who plummeted us, practicing their blocking patterns. We played a brief scrimmage toward the end of practice. The first string played offense with the first stringers who played both ways being replaced by us scrubs on defense. I got to play defensive right end. Stan and Del tried to run me over blocking for Bobby Champ, but I made them look foolish by sidestepping them. I just used their momentum to push them to the ground when they threw themselves at me. The runner had a choice of trying to run around me or running smack into Jon who had filled in the hole when he saw the play develop. He chose to run around me and I tackled him easily.

Coach Adamson shouted. "Way to go Harris, that's the way to play defensive end. I keep telling you defensive ends to box in to stop the end runs. Harris did it right."

At least he knew my name.

Del said, "Way to go Hermie."

I looked at him and smiled.

"Katie sure is a pretty girl isn't she," I said.

That took the wind out of his sails.

Then Jon said, "Bitch'n play Mo, even though the blocking was bad, it was a great play."

That added to Del's misery.

The coach blew his whistle and called for wind sprints to end the practice. Maybe I'd get to play a lot in the next game Saturday. If I didn't play, what the hell, there was Saturday night and Katie Gutierrez.

That evening Pop showed me an ad for a 1948 Buick in the weekly village newspaper. The seller wanted $200.00. It wasn't exactly what I was looking for. I wanted something I could customize like a 1952 Ford. Pop said he would throw in the extra 50 bucks as I only had $150 in my savings. He didn't want me to drive a hot rod. He wanted me in a more sedate car that would keep me from speeding and getting into trouble. The car was an automatic, another thing he liked. He knew that the stick shift encouraged kids to race because they like the feel of shifting up through the gears.

My car, a slush wagon, at least the big back seat made a great make out spot.

"How about I call and we look at it tomorrow. If it checks out okay, you can buy it," Pop said.

My mind flashed to Katie. "Sure," I said.

Now I'd have my own wheels to drive Katie to the dance. Bitch'n.

Mom, as if reading my mind chimed in, "A girl named Katie called you. She asked that you call her back after practice."

I disliked calling anybody from the single dial phone we kept in the living room, especially a girl about a date. Mom and Pop would sit right there, all ears. I shifted my body uncomfortably to shield my voice. I called her and set up the time, about 6:30 pm. That way I could clean-up and change after the game. She told me she and her girl friends planned to watch the game. She sounded excited, cool. And me, able to drive us to the dance in my own car.

I knew for sure that Mom could read my mind, because when I hung up she said, "Now that you have a car, you had better not be getting any girls pregnant."

Dad said, "Oh leave him alone. Why do you assume that?"

"It's my first date with her. If I kiss her goodnight, I'll be lucky," I said.

That night I fell asleep late. My mind raced over Katie Gutierrez's soft brown eyes warm brown skin, and every other part of her imaginable.

We bought the car Tuesday. I called Rich to say that I intended to drive myself to school the next day. I told him about it - not exactly a hot rod but big, great for making out. I drove it to school the next few days, relishing the feeling. The big five checked it out when I pulled up at school. They pointed out the roomy back seat. Katie blushed. It made her golden brown skin even more appealing.

12

The game Saturday against a small school in Vista went well. I got to play more than Del, which must have really pissed him off. Stan lurched his way through the game playing ineffectively. Neither team had scored by the fourth quarter because Vista played as bad as Coronado. Then with only a few minutes to go in the game, Jon intercepted a botched pass play deep in their territory and virtually skipped in to score the only touchdown of the game. Our kicker missed the extra point leaving the final score at six to nothing.

Thoughts of Katie kept popping into my head during the game. The win excited the fans in the stands more than me. Other things occupied my mind. I hurried through my shower ignoring Del's dirty looks. In the locker room, Jon basked in the glory of his winning play. I headed home to change and put on some cool clothes for the dance.

I pulled up at Katie's mansion near the beach, still tired and sore from the game. She answered the bell and invited me in. She wore a cocktail dress, which showed off her figure and a bit of cleavage. Her modestly displayed breasts were impossible to ignore. My post game soreness, disappeared forgotten, like my tiredness. I floated lightheaded through the introductions to her parents. Katie shied up, charming the hell out of me. Her parents both spoke with strong accents and beamed at their daughter.

I stood in the entrance and looked around at the house. The heavy wood front door opened to a foyer with lots of stained wood moldings. A Spanish style mansion, that's the best way to describe the place. Besides her parents, a diminutive squat little Mexican woman stood just outside the foyer where a hall led off somewhere. She stood ready to bustle about as directed. The center of the foyer looked into the living room, which was about as large as my folk's whole house. On one side of the room stood a large black grand piano, a marble copy of Venus de Milo occupied a little alcove nearby. Various sofas and straight back chairs, some with gold gilding, filled the room. They didn't look like anyone ever sat on them. I figured there must be another part of the house where the family took off their shoes and relaxed.

"We expect her home by midnight young man," her dad said, and patted me on the arm in a way that implied he was kidding but at the same time, that he meant it. I understood exactly.

"Yes sir," I said.

When we got outside Katie started yakking on and on. She talked almost nonstop until we got to the gym. We saw Jill and Sharon Galloway. Both looked sexy. Katie looked the sexiest in her dress. Her body seemed ready to burst out, yet it covered her modestly. I kept glancing at her as we talked with her friends. Jill Hankins didn't seem uneasy at all, but I felt uncomfortable remembering Jill on the beach that night. Jill's date, another senior, stood around awkward, not knowing what to say. She invited him, I am not sure why, maybe to impress her mom. Sharon's boyfriend Jim Ready escorted her. A brainy guy, he also ran track. He looked sort of tall and gawky. He and Sharon talked about some physics problem from school. They were lab partners. They looked comfortable together, but their relationship didn't appear to sizzle. Oh well, Katie and I sure sizzled. Bitch'n.

A couple of junior girls accompanied Bobby Champ and Jim Nelson. Stan and his closest sidekick, Del weren't there. Probably no girl wanted to be seen with those pseudo hoods. Joe Carlson usually showed up outside later. He wouldn't miss a chance to sell some Mary Jane.

Katie felt warm dancing the slow dances. She squeezed my hand when I pressed against her. We sat at a table and sipped soft drinks between dances. At the intermission, the band took a break and I asked her outside to get some fresh air. Outside the gym, a light chill filled the stillness. Soft clouds from offshore moved overhead. We walked around the corner and across the street toward the open field the school used for PE. A small set of bleachers stood near the street on the quiet, grassy grounds.

"It's pretty at night," she said.

"It's nice. Look how part of the moon shows through the clouds," I said.

"I'm cold." She held herself in a hug.

I put my arm around her and pulled her close.

"Better," she said.

I kissed her then and felt her respond. We continued over to the bleachers, sat down, and necked. She seemed to like it. She definitely didn't hold back. I longed to caress her all over but restrained myself and just kept my arms around her waist.

"I'm having a lot of fun with you tonight, Mo, but we can't date after this," she said. "I plan to start college without a boyfriend. If I wanted one you'd be nice, but you're just a sophomore. It wouldn't work out. We move in different circles. Anyway my parents want me to find a nice Spanish boyfriend."

That didn't surprise me. What did surprise me was that she came out and said it. I knew she planned this date to end Del's infatuation with her, but this felt like another date, like the one I had with Jill. I hoped it would end the same way.

"So what makes you think, I'd want to date a senior chick like you, just because you're cute?" I said.

"Because of this." She kissed me open mouth, tongue, everything and she moved her right leg up and over my left leg right between my knees. Bitch'n.

The necking session only lasted ten minutes or so.

"The band will be starting, we better go back," she said.

I couldn't argue with her. Anyway, you can't get much sitting out in the open like that.

"I guess so," I said.

She giggled and said, "Don't' worry, we'll have time later."

Katie stopped in the ladies room to freshen up. I didn't think she needed any freshening up. I decided to check myself out in the restroom mirror and maybe take a mint to be ready for the next make-out session.

When I came out, Katie hadn't come out of the girl's room yet, probably giggling with her friends in there. I saw Joe Carlson with the De La Puente kid. That seemed like an odd combination. Then I saw Coach Adamson chatting with them both. Coach often chaperoned our school dances. The coach pretty much ignored any drunkenness and just watched out for any fights, which made him popular at dances. I could understand him talking to the little Mexican because the kid played football, but why Carlson? Then I spotted the older Mexican standing near the door. In the dim light, I edged closer to the group.

"Be careful Joe," the coach said. "I don't want this to blow up."

"No, no, no, we'll just stand outside." Carlson said.

Then the coach moved off toward the front of the gym as the band came back. It struck up the Everly Brothers hit, *All I have to do is Dream*. Katie came out with the other girls, took my hand and led me out to the dance floor with a little smile. She pushed herself tight against me to dance. I didn't have to pull her close like before. My hand slid down to rest on the swell of her hips. She squeezed my hand. I pressed her hips against mine. She squeezed my hand harder. Bitch'n.

The dance ended and some stupid fast dance started, *Rock'n Roll'n Rover* or something. Katie still wanted to dance so I obliged. I'd rather hold her close in a slow one.

A. J. Converse

Now, outside our little world of dancing, I took a look around.

Coach stood near the band looking over the crowd. What did it mean when he said he didn't want *this to blow up?* That struck me as unusual. I knew he made political moves in picking his regular players, concentrating on the elite sons of high level Navy Officers in town and possibly other key people. Then I realized he made De La Puente a starter because of the kid's father. Jon played linebacker better than that little shit. Moreover, Jon was bigger and hit harder. The coach seemed to be conspiring with Carlson, who pedaled drugs - why the coach? He should be the last guy to huddle with Carlson, the way he preached training rules. Maybe the talk around school the previous year about an affair involving the Coach and a senior girl had some truth. What kind of teacher does that? His player choices implied that he was either corrupt or stupid. He wasn't stupid. My suspicions deepened.

I knew thugs started first with marijuana, then move to other drugs, like heroin. I had seen *The Man with the Golden Arm* a couple years before. That stuff was dangerous. People died from heroin. I realized then, that not all authority figures were honest and trustworthy. Pop's talk with me about his philosophy and our neighbor Mr. Morris, hit home. The coach seemed to be one of those people in the great fuzziness of right and wrong, who continued to get away with breaking the rules.

The band started playing slow songs and I forgot about philosophy. Katie's body pressed against me. I could feel her breasts and imagined her nipples against me. When her thigh brushed against my manhood, it focused all my attention on that sensation. After some more steamy close dancing, about 10 o'clock, I asked Katie to go for a ride with me. She knew that meant some heavier necking and making out, and she seemed excited by it. She agreed right away. We left Jill and Sharon talking animatedly with their dates at one of the tables. Compared to those guys, I had a hot date tonight.

Coach Adamson stood just outside the gym, near the door. I noticed him with Sergio De La Puente as we walked out. De La Puente handed him something that looked like a wad of money. The coach quickly pocked it. That's what I saw wasn't it? I wasn't sure.

"Did you see that?" I asked Katie.

"I saw it. That Cholo handed the coach something."

"Huh?" I said. She had used a word I had never heard before.

"Oh, Cholo that's Spanish. It means a Mexican Indian or sort of a thug."

"That new Mexican student is a thug?" I said.

"His father has connections with bad people. He's a Mexican citizen but he lives in Imperial Beach."

"How do you know?" I said.

"My father knows a lot of government officials in Mexico. He and Mom told me to stay away from his son at school. They said he is Cholo."

"Hey, are you Mexican or Spanish?" I said.

She told me that Mexican referred to a citizen of Mexico. Most are quite dark because they are the same as those we call Indian in the US. She was an American, not a Mexican because she was a US citizen. Her Mother, a full-blooded Aztec Indian, grew up in Mexico City. That's where she met and married Mr. Gutierrez, a rich Spaniard with dual US and Mexican citizenship. He came from an old family that originated in Spain. She said that Spaniards still controlled most land and wealth in Mexico. Many Americans disliked the Indians of Mexico whether they had become American citizens or not, so her family preferred to refer to themselves as Spanish. I learned more about her and Mexicans in that little explanation than I had ever understood before. Part Indian, no problem, if I cared about her skin color, it was to regard it as especially attractive, and her body, wow.

"Joe Carlson sells marijuana along with a couple of Mexicans from Imperial Beach. It looks like the coach is involved and probably De La Puente." I said.

"I hope you stay away from that crowd, Mo," she said. "I think they've hooked Stan Huffman and Del Webber."

"Yea, I wonder where they are tonight." I said.

"I think they're at the beach smoking reefers with Joe's Mexican friends." She said.

"How do you know all that?"

"Well Stan called Liz to ask her out again and Liz told him no. So he said, *well that does it. I guess I'll just go to the beach and smoke weed with Del.* He didn't mean cigarettes. He was trying to make her feel guilty, but Liz knows how he thinks. She told him to bug off."

I laughed. It sounded so funny the way she said it. I couldn't picture goody-goody Liz saying something like that.

"I can picture Jill saying that, but not Liz," I said.

Katie smiled.

"I won't have to tell you to bug off after tonight will I Mo," she said. "This is just one date. My parents won't let me see an Anglo boy for long. They want me to eventually marry a rich Spaniard."

I laughed.

"I don't kiss and tell. Anyway you're too old for me and I am too young to start any permanent girlfriend boyfriend thing."

"Jill told me that about you," she said.

"What else did Jill tell you?"

She just giggled.

I played it cool, but she sure would be nice to have as a girlfriend. I didn't tell her that. I wanted to keep things light, no discussion of feelings. I didn't want to cool her off and lose any opportunity with her. I shut the heck up and kissed her just as we got to my car. She responded in such a way, I knew that I had made the right call.

We drove the short trip out to the beach. I picked a dark spot on the street near the fence by the North Island Naval Air Base and parked the car. We were making out sprawled on the front seat, already further along then I ever thought I could get with her, when I heard a knock on the window. Shit, I thought it was a cop breaking us up. He'd make us move just when things were really getting hot. It wasn't a cop.

"Get the fuck ... out of that car now ... I'm gonna kick your ass," Del sputtered.

He was already loopy on marijuana and beer. Stan loomed like a large shadow next to him. Barely visible in the starlight, the two jerks spoiled for a fight.

Katie said, "Give it up Del, I'm with Mo now, get lost."

Snarling, Del opened her door and grabbed her out of the car. Her sweater had been pulled up, her bra was askew, and she had no time to fix that. Del's eyes were wide with fury. Before he could say or do anything, Katie slapped him hard on the face. I shot out of the car behind her and threw Del to the ground.

Out of nowhere, Stan sucker-punched me on the side of my head. I landed hard on the pavement, my head pounding. I saw black and almost went out. As I struggled to rise, I saw Katie swing at Stan's face with her high-heeled shoe. She caught him good and he grabbed his face.

"Fuck," he said, "you bitch, I'll pound you for that." He doubled his fists as he moved toward her.

93

Still groggy, I forced myself to stand up and kick Stan in the nuts. It was almost too easy. He bent over holding his crotch and swearing. He was bigger than me. I had to take him fast before he could get any momentum. I kicked him again, this time my foot smashed his face. He went down. I kicked him in the kidney and turned to Del who had stood up. The little chicken took one look at me and ran away. I turned back to see Katie flailing Stan with her shoe. Stan held his arms up, but many of her blows landed.

"You think you're gonna pound me, you gringo bastard. My dad will have you killed if you ever touch me," she screamed.

She had lost her perfect English and reverted to a Spanish accent as she hit him again and again.

I grabbed her arm and said, "I think Stan has had enough tiger." I couldn't help grinning at her.

The strength in her arms surprised me. Her eyes gleamed and her golden skin flushed dark with excitement. Then she laughed, not a girlish giggle but a full robust guffaw.

"You've never seen me get mad before, have you?" She said.

"I always thought you were a quiet, shy little Mexican, oops I mean Spanish girl."

"I'm tough when I'm mad."

"Must be from your mother's side of the family," I said.

Stan walked away holding the side of his head. He was drunk and had just been beaten senseless by me and a hot Latin chick with a temper. If he were smart, he'd head home to sleep it off. Del was long gone.

"That ought to stop Del from chasing me." Katie said.

I opened the car door for her. She pushed back the front seat and climbed into the back. She reached out and pulled me in with her.

"Now, she said. I will show you my Aztec soul."

Hot damn.

It was bitch'n. She responded when my hand moved between her thighs. She moved her hand to touch me and began to moan and hump her hips. We got lost together in a rising tide of passion. Our movements quickened. She kissed me hard and long, until she seemed to shudder. She relaxed, snuggling close, gently moving her hand away from me. She was satisfied – not me. She kissed me gently.

"That's enough for tonight, Mo." She breathed the words softly and squeezed my hand. It left me wanting more, but that was as much as I would get that night.

We stopped back at the dance about 11:30 so Katie could freshen up in the restroom. I waited outside, remembering Katie's beautiful body, smell and passion.

A less agreeable smell reached me. About a dozen kids gathered just outside with Joe Carlson and the De La

Puente kid, buying marijuana. Crap, I thought sleaze, drugs and losers. Just as that gloomy thought washed over me, a giggling Katie and Liz walked out of the ladies room. One look at them and I thought well, maybe not all the kids are losers. Katie gave me a big kiss in front of everyone, Liz, the druggies and all. Then we went back to the car.

"We need to talk before you bring me home." She said.

In the car, she told me she got carried away by the excitement of the fight and claimed she had never gone that far.

"A one-time thing," she said. "Don't pursue me after this."

She was quite firm for a shy Spanish girl. At that precise point, if she had given me any encouragement, I would have been hopelessly snowed.

"Don't compare me with that dork Dell," I said. "I don't kiss and tell."

Some weight came off my shoulders when I realized I was still a free man. Along with the relief came regret, she was one hot number. This sex stuff really twisted up my head. I drove her home just before midnight and walked her to the door. She gave me a polite kiss goodnight. I pictured her old man just behind the door.

13

What a run of luck. I whipped two of the so-called hard guys in school, well, with a little help from Katie, and I got to third base with one of the Big Five. Bitch'n.

I decided to push my good luck and stopped at the police station on the way home. I walked in and told the watch officer that I noticed some students smoking marijuana at the gym and I thought that they ought to send a car there and put a stop to it.

He was a skinny guy with blond hair with a voice deeper than I expected. He laughed and said, "Hell we don't have marijuana in our town. That stuff only turns up in San Diego."

So much for the town's finest. I had that gloomy feeling again. Things at the school would never get back to the fun times once drugs made their way in. The hard stuff always follows marijuana. No more pretty girls and cool guys, just scags and scuzzbags at my school. Crap.

When I got home, I opened the door quietly so not to wake up Mom and Pop. But Mom heard me anyway and said from the bedroom, "Did you have a good time dear?"

"Yea."

"That's nice."

Cool, I didn't want to chat about my date or the douche bags selling drugs. My mind spun from Katie's soft body to images of the drug crap.

BITCH'N

I dragged my ass out of bed at 4:00 am and struggled through my route. As I finished up and rode my motor bike into the lot next to my parent's duplex, I noticed a big new Cadillac with its parking lights on. The doors opened and Sergio De La Puente, Stan, Del, and Joe Carlson stepped out. They swaggered up to me as I put down the kickstand. *Crap.* I swallowed and a little pit of fear deep inside turned into the beginnings of a rage. If they were going to gang up on me, they would pay a price. Then Deak Morris stepped out of his unit. His screen door slammed. He sauntered over to where we stood.

"Any problem Harris," he asked.

The four-pseudo hoods were startled. They turned and saw Boswain Mate Deacon Morris standing in front of them stretched to his full five feet, six inch height and outfitted in his Bo 'swain's pipe and dress whites. Big Stan's bravado crumpled and he seemed to shrink his six foot two inch frame to three inches in front of my neighbor.

"I think these four youths are about to go home to their mommies and daddies," I said.

My rage evaporated as suddenly as it had emerged. The four hoods sort of slid away toward their car and eased out of the lot, their eyes avoiding my glance. Bitch'n.

"Thanks, Mr. Morris," I said.

"If those high school punks give you anymore trouble just let me know kid," Then he drove off in his old Ford coup.

I slept until 11:00 when Rich called and asked me to pick up the guys – some kind of trouble with his car. We planned to spend some time at the beach, if it was warm enough. I made the rounds and picked everyone up, Larson last. He grinned as he popped into the car.

"Hey Mo, what's this I heard about you making out with Katie Gutierrez on the bleachers last night?"

He grinned.

"Well she was appreciative of the date. I'll just say that. We had a run-in with Stan Huffman and Del Webber last night. Stan sucker punched me. Then Katie attacked him with her shoe and I kicked him in the nuts. He took a good beating from us both. Del ran."

"Del actually ran?" he said.

"Yea, he's a real wimp. Katie wielding her shoe scared him. She turns into a tiger when she gets riled up. They tried to even the score this morning when I came home from my route, but they ran into my neighbor."

I laughed.

"He's only about five six, but he sure scared the shit out of them. They even had Carlson and the De la Puente kid with them."

That got them off the subject of my degree of success with Katie. They said that they spent the evening drinking beer at the beach and picked up some chicks that were staying at the Del Coronado Hotel. Down from Burbank for a weekend get-away with their rich parents, the chicks

99

were fast. Hampton and Jon got laid. Larson didn't quite go that far and Rich's big smile said everything. They bought Larson some mints to overpower his beer breath. That and the lipstick on his collar got him by his old man when he got home. His old man figured he was making out, and not drinking beer.

"So are you going to see Katie again?" Rich asked.

"Nope, she made that clear last night." Then I changed the subject to Jon's game winning interception the previous night.

The football team managed to improve in spite of the coach. By Thanksgiving, we had a four and four record. Our last game was scheduled the Saturday after Thanksgiving against our archrival Imperial Beach. Our schools were the same size so the teams were evenly matched, except the coaches. Their coach played the best players, so they had a six and two record.

I got to play. Before now, I hadn't ever had a pass thrown anywhere near me. This time our quarterback actually threw the ball near me. I caught it. There was no one between the goal line and me. I ran like hell expecting a hit any minute from behind. Like a dream, I heard the crowd roar, time seemed to stop. The goal looked as if I would never get to it. I seemed to float, covering the 50 yards to the end zone in a daze. We actually kicked the extra point successfully. Bitch'n. After that, the possession went back and forth without a score until halftime. As I ran into the gym with the team, I ran by the big five. They all yelled "Way to go Hermie!"

In the second half, Imperial Beach got a touchdown. Del caused it. Del was so wimpy at defensive end; he couldn't box in the blockers and make the play either run out of bounds or make the runner cut in toward our linebackers. The blockers actually spun him around while he tried to hold them off and avoid being hurt. The little halfback turned the corner and ran 40 yards into the end zone. Fortunately, they missed the point after, so the score was 7 to 6.

On the kickoff, Stan received a short kick and lumbered a couple yards to the forty where the Imperial Beach team tackled him. He got up off the ground and strutted around as if he was Jim Brown or something. Jon got in the game, got the ball, and broke though the one surprised linebacker between him and a touchdown. He scampered for it. A couple of the other team's players caught up with him near the end zone. The picture in the Coronado paper the next day showed him running into the end zone carrying two Imperial Beach players trying desperately to bring him down. That was his moment. The coach left Jon and I in the game on defense for the rest of the game. Coronado had no more scores, but neither did Imperial Beach, so we won 14 to 6.

After a couple days of popularity, the hoopla faded for me. My TD run was forgotten. Football, I concluded, wasn't worth the effort, but Jon played for the rest of his high school years.

14

Near Christmas, the word spread of a Saturday night house party. A senior chick, whose parents looked the other way when kids drank at their house, planned it. She lived in a large mansion near the beach. Her parents always retreated to their bedroom suite during a party. About 80 kids could be expected to show up at a party like this. Of course, the guys and I planned to attend. We wouldn't miss it.

The night of the party, I drove Larson and Jon in my Buick and Rich drove Hampton. We drove because we wanted our cars available to go out and get a tap. Anyway, the cars would be useful for chicks, especially my Buick with its big back seat. We arrived about the same time. We reconnoitered the huge mansion to get the lay of the land, before going out looking for a tap.

The fog rolled in and warmed the winter night making it comfortable for my new letter sweater. The landscaped lot insulated the main house from the outside world. Large jade plants near the sidewalk created a natural fence surrounding the yard. Bougainvillea in key locations along the house walls, shielded windows and blocked the view of activities in the yard. A few ground lights along the walkways lit a dim path on the inside grounds. Little alcoves and arbors of banana trees and bamboo showed great promise for places to make out. Bitch'n.

Although we could barely hear the music from the sidewalk outside, a wall of music hit us as we entered the house. *Stagger Lee* blasted out of a record player. A mass of kids filled the room. A keg of beer in a corner attracted a line of eager partiers. Some kids drank hard stuff from little paper cups – free booze. We wouldn't need a tap.

As I walked over to the keg, I noticed Sharon Galloway standing there with her brother. I didn't see her boyfriend, Jim Ready. Not much of a socializer, Sharon's brother did appear at some parties. None of the other big five chicks attended. Sharon looked a little lonely. Most boys stayed away from her because she had a boyfriend and because she normally liked to talk about science. My success with Jill and Katie made me feel studly. I decided to strike up a conversation and ambled over toward her.

Down to earth, Sharon talked to underclassmen even if their fathers lived in the enlisted housing area. She didn't flirt. She wasn't shy, just a friendly unassuming girl with a sensual body and a brain. Her Navy brat, steady boyfriend earned top grades at school just like her. Her own father was a Navy Commander. I worked hard to get B's and C's in college prep courses but school came easy to her. Sharon and her boyfriend loved science, physics and that kind of stuff. I'd heard that she planned to attend Stanford University when she graduated. It was her well-formed body that got my attention.

"Merry Christmas," I said.

"Oh hi Hermie," she said.

I winced at that and she noticed.

She corrected herself saying, "Oh, I mean hi Mo." Then she smiled.

"Where's Ready tonight?" I said.

"We decided not to date anymore."

In my experience, if a girl decided not to date anymore, it meant things were getting too hot and heavy for her. Probably Ready wanted to go all-the-way and she didn't. Maybe that left an opening for this stud. "You're on the loose," I said.

"Oh Mo I wouldn't say that. I'm just checking things out at this party. I'm no party girl. Besides Janie is my friend."

Janie's parents owned the place.

"Can I get you a beer?" I said.

"Okay, sure."

Someone turned off the overhead light. The room darkened. A little table lamp in the corner cast the only light. I fumbled in the dark as I picked up a paper cup and poured out the beer, trying not to make a big head. Someone had removed most of the furniture from this large game room. A pool table remained in the center, probably too heavy to move. Several chairs and a couple couches were pushed to the sides of the room. I wondered how many chicks would get planked on that pool table. The image and Jon's new word for sex made me chuckle to myself. I noticed Hampton talking earnestly to a sophomore girl in the corner. He still had interests other than getting drunk, a good sign. Jon, Larson and Rich had moved to some other part of the house. Music came from another room. I didn't see the town hoods, Stan and Del and their buddies. Ominous, I thought, because if they came at the start it meant they came for fun. Not being at the party now, meant that they were on the beach somewhere smoking marijuana and drinking beer and god knows what else. They'd show up late in a belligerent mood. I realized then that I was a partier, not a hard guy. I didn't look forward to a fight these days.

I carried the beer over to Sharon. Her brother stood off in a corner talking to some other chick. Sharon bounced on her toes and took her beer.

"I heard you're going to Stanford to study physics next year." I said.

"Huh, oh yea, probably. This beer tastes good. I only drank once before in my life."

"I always wondered about the speed of light. How come nothing can go faster?" I missed her cue to change the subject.

"Now you sound like Jim."

I finally got the message and put on my best listening face.

"Do you want to talk about it?"

"Jim and I've been friends since junior high school. We liked to talk and argue about the universe, life on other planets and stuff like that. We were just friends, not much kissing and stuff like that. He wasn't interested."

BITCH'N

It hit me... oops he's queer. I never thought of that before. I wondered why the two never touched each other like other high school couples did. So I asked.

"What's he queer or something?"

She laughed in a sardonic way.

"I don't know, maybe it's me. I don't appeal to him." she said.

"I doubt it is you, unless he's blind."

I guess her brother talked her into coming to the party at the last minute. She wore white short-shorts, little tennis shoes with no socks and a sleeveless white blouse. She had a sweater draped over her shoulders. Occasionally, as we talked, I peeked at the armholes of the sleeveless blouse. Beautiful little breasts in some sort of half bra peeked out.

"Get me another beer and take me for a walk." She said.

A walk, cool, my mind filled with lust. Well, maybe she wanted to take a walk so she wouldn't feel like a fish in a bowl. Guys eyed her, mostly seniors, and looked me up and down. The looks implied who the hell was I talking to a senior chick and where was Jim Ready anyway. I got my head under control and got two more beers.

We went out on the sidewalk and walked around the grounds, which occupied the whole block. Normally chilly near the beach at night, it was warmer than usual this time. A fog had rolled in, full of relatively warm air. We walked in what seemed to be our own little world, a cocoon of fog. We could see just a few feet either way and our voices were muffled.

Sharon had been blabbing on and on how bad she felt breaking up with Ready. Finally, she said there just wasn't any physical attraction there. I could have told her that. I just listened without comment. She slipped her sweater down and tied it around her waist. I endured the blah, blah, blah and enjoyed the little peeks her sleeveless blouse gave me of her breasts. She kept leaning into me so I took the hint and put my arm around her. That took away the little peeks I'd had before but I liked the feel of her leaning against me. Bitch'n.

As we came around a corner, a new Cadillac appeared suddenly, as if it had just materialized, idling by the curb. The little Mexican transfer student, De La Puente, and his old man sat in the front. The two rough looking Mexicans that hung out with Joe Carlson lounged in the back seat.

Drug dealers follow the market, I thought.

"Isn't that the new transfer student in that car?" I said.

"So?" she said.

"I think they're selling weed and using Joe Carlson and to some extent Stan Huffman and his buddies to do it. I think they're paying off the coach too."

"Huh, I don't think so..." she said. "Weed, what's that?" She said, wide eyed.

Sharon was a goody-goody. So, I didn't press it. I had other things on my mind anyway. Those nice little breasts, which peeked out at me now and then, were two of those things. As we came around the back of the house, we saw some activity on the porch. An older guy poured out something in little cups. The same little cups I had seen earlier.

Sharon said, "Let's see what it is."

We went in the back gate and lined up. The older brother of the chick whose parents owned the place poured out something called "192." Sharon seemed to want some, so I got two cups filled with one inch of the stuff. I tasted it and it was awful, like lighter fluid or something. The guy pouring called it *white lighting*, nearly straight alcohol. I'm a stud, I thought, so I sipped it. Sharon sipped some, made a face then gulped it down. Wow. We went inside from the back door through the kitchen where a big tub of ice held beer, no soft drinks. Sharon asked for a beer. I reached in the tub and got one.

"Let's share it," she said. She took a sip.

"Good, the beer kills the taste of that 192 stuff," she said.

"Yea, it's pretty potent," I said, taking another sip of the white lightning.

Then she handed me the beer and said, "Take some beer then just drink the 192 down. I don't think it's good to sip it."

I did. I wondered where she had learned that.

She stumbled a bit and I realized she was getting high.

"This is fun," she said, and pressed me against the counter and kissed me.

"It's getting better and better," I said and took another sip of beer.

She sent me to get more of the 192. When I got back, she pressed against me again then took her cup. We each downed our second cup in one gulp and took long swigs on our beers.

She was giggling.

"Let's go in there," I said pointing to a bedroom.

She grinned and nodded conspiratorially as we stumbled toward the door. Inside a couple was already using the bed.

"It's being used," I said.

"Looks like fun," she said. "Get me - another cup of that 192, Hermie."

She was high now. She could handle only one more drink without passing out, the last thing I wanted to deal with tonight. However, another cup might loosen her up even more. I got the booze. I got just one cup, figuring we could share it. She moved close, holding my hand with both of hers as the guy poured it out. It looked like white lightning to me, but I doubted he made it himself. Then I saw in big letters on the bottle peaking out of the paper bag, *192*. She sipped it this time, then took a sip of the beer and gave me a sip of each.

BITCH'N

"Come on - you have to share this with me. I can't - drink it all." She said.

She slurred her words now.

I could walk home if I really got polluted, or maybe Rich would drive me home and I could pick up the Buick in the morning ... or something. Things weren't too clear. I was getting Sharon on the rebound but I didn't care. She was almost 18, old enough to know what she was doing. She led me to a couple of rooms but they all seemed to be occupied. Hampton and that little sophomore chick occupied one, all spread out and clutching each other on the bed.

"Jimmy would never do this... he, he... He'd have gotten mad...went home if I ever suggested making out...sex..." She said.

She was crocked, she was ready, but having sex with a drunken girl wasn't exactly what I had in mind. What the hell, I was drunk too, probably...yea. What if she regretted it in the morning...what if I did? She was taking advantage of me... a younger guy. That's what I told myself anyway.

"Don't worry I'm...not that drunk...know what I am doing," she said, as if reading my mind.

A bit crocked myself, I believed her. We opened another bedroom door, the bed piled high with coats – no lovers. The partiers used it as a closet. I pulled Sharon inside and closed the door.

She whispered. "Lock it."

It had an old-fashioned hook type lock, which I located and locked. Her passion pushed her all over me, she touched, kissed, fumbled with my belt. I guided her to the bed. We crawled onto the hill of coats.

"You...ever done this before?" I said.

"No... never done it...never had a boy get to...second base... well maybe third base. But I want it...tonight..."

Her voice trailed off. I hoped she wouldn't pass out on me. We piled onto the bed on top of the coats and wrestled with our clothes, and then with my pants down, and her shorts off, we slipped off the bed, landing on the floor, a bunch of coats all around us. The noise must have carried because someone started pounding on the door. I pulled up my pants; she found her shorts and got them on.

"Come on," I said.

We stumbled out of the room, giggling. Fortunately, the hallway was dark, because the person pounding on the door was Sharon's brother who wanted to get his coat. We flashed by him before he realized that the couple in the room included his sister.

We headed outside.

"Where're...we going?"

She staggered along. I staggered too but she stuck to me, holding onto my hand with one hand and carrying the beer in the other. We already finished the cup of 192. We wasted no time and climbed into the back seat of the

Buick. She had sex eagerly, wild, and hungry. I entered her; too drunk to worry about taking advantage of her inebriated condition.

After, she said, "Hermie, you may not believe me…that was my first time."

At least she knew who I was. She didn't think she had just screwed Jim Ready. She seemed a little more sober.

"You told me that already," I said.

Then came the little speech about how it was just a one time thing, I was just a sophomore and she didn't want any entanglements and I had better not spread it all around school, blah, blah, blah. The speech was familiar.

We eased out of the car. Sharon threw up all over the street. That sobered her. We went back inside and found a bathroom. She shied up when she had me help fasten her bra after we washed up. I hadn't taken any precautions. I started to worry about that.

"We don't need you to get pregnant," I said.

"I don't think I can…it's is the wrong time of month… oh… I should have been more careful," she said.

"Chalk it up to the 192," I said.

I wasn't sure what the right time of month was, just before the period, probably. She knew, I hoped. The picture of me with a pregnant Sharon Galloway flashed in my mind. Crap, I hardly knew her. What had I done? I had a flash of insight of how screwed up a guy's life could get. Hell, I told myself, I just got laid. How could that be a problem? I'll be more careful next time. But the nagging point of fear was still there, bugging me.

"I'll have to double check tomorrow. My mom gave me a big medical book on my 16th birthday to read about reproduction. I'll check that…oh dear…" she sighed.

"God, I hope you're right," I said.

About 10 o'clock true to form, the Stan Huffman pack showed up drunk and mean. Del staggered around smashed out of his mind. He lurched into the living room and passed out on a couch. Stan and Joe Carlson maneuvered around the room shaking down kids for money. They just shook down kids to be macho - extortion. Either one could buy anything they wanted. The local cops wouldn't do anything about it even if someone reported them. High school punks, not a big deal, is the way they would look at it. Some guys just slinked out of the room. The ones that Joe and Stan caught generally coughed up a couple of bucks.

"Come on man," I heard Carlson say, "We need it for beer."

The kid said, "But there's free beer here."

Carlson grabbed his shirt, "Are you gonna fuck with me you little bastard?"

That was enough for him. He gave Joe all the money he had in his wallet. The two hoods started angling toward us. I observed them calmly; we had a history. Anyway, I was crocked, I had just gotten laid, no problem, I could handle a couple of sleaze-balls.

***

Joe saw the Harris kid. That bastard always had some chick. He even hustled the senior chicks. Girls started avoiding Joe about the time he started smoking weed and doing other drugs. They shunned him now. Joe told himself he didn't give a fuck. Anyway, he could get as much ass as he wanted down in TJ. Stan and Dell smoked marijuana. Soon he would get them on the hard drugs. He was building a following that would maintain his own growing addiction. So what if they were his only remaining friends in the school. They wouldn't let him down. He was getting them into some cool drugs and soon more would join his gang, chicks too. Sergio and his old man stocked some ludes out in their car. That's what he wanted, ludes. Strong arm a few more kids, get some ludes and crash. That's what he wanted. Maybe get Stan and Dell to try one.

Joe knew he couldn't do drugs forever. Some part of him realized life was a downhill slide from here, but he didn't give a damn. First the beer, then he needed weed, now only the ludes quieted his rage and stopped the voice. He'd enjoy life as long as he could get his drugs. His parents...Loretta screamed at him and the old man whacked him. Fuck his parents and fuck the world.

He could handle these party pukes easy. He'd start friendly like, giving the wimps a cool way to agree to give him money. They'd think they looked cool, helping him, a cool cat. If that failed, threatening a beating did the trick. Part of him hoped that some jerk would resist. He liked a

114

fight. He always kicked ass. And here was Harris; he always wanted to beat the shit out of him.

***

Stan got to me first. "Hey Mo, how about helping us out."

"Which way did you come in, Stanley," I chuckled. Aww, the power of booze. Sharon didn't share my aplomb. She cowered behind me.

Stan bore in close and said, "Very funny, asshole. Give us some bread."

His eyes red from smoking marijuana and drinking, his breath reeking of barf, he leaned on me.

"What drugs are you gonna buy from those Mexicans out in the car?" I said.

"What Mexicans? What're you talking about asshole?" Stan pushed his hard guy act.

"They've got Carlson on the hard stuff. Look at him. He's busting apart at the seams. You getting hooked too?" I said.

He pushed his face next to mine. I grimaced from the barf smell but I stood my ground.

"You smell like you've been licking toilets."

"Cough up the money jerk, or I'll pound you," he said.

Playing it cool, I stared unflinchingly, reached down, and grabbed his nuts hard, right through his Levis. His face turned white. I squeezed as hard as I could and lifted him to his toes by his testicles. He bent down with a twisted face as he balanced in pain on his tiptoes. He couldn't talk. He just sort of squeaked while he tried to pull my hand away.

"Jerk?" I said while staring him straight in the eyes.

I should've been watching Carlson. He hit me hard in the kidney knocking my wind out. I folded, holding my gut and loosening my grip on Stan.

Sharon screamed, "stop, help."

The host's brother rushed into the room and shouted, "Get out or I'll call the police."

"Okay mother fucker, get your ass outside and you better bring money," Carlson said.

Then the stoned asshole headed outside with Stan.

My side throbbed with pain but I managed to growl, "I'll bring my fists, you pussy."

I watched them go out the back. Holding my side in pain, I grabbed Sharon's hand and led her out the front to my car and we took off in the fog. God knows what they did next. They were too stoned to spend much time looking for me. Sharon, scared and excited, clutched me close. Jazzed myself, I drove to the beach and parked at a dark spot in the fog. It was thick as pea soup by the beach. Even sober, Stan and Joe couldn't find us.

Sharon whispered, "In the back seat."

That's when we screwed a second time. Wahoo, a double. Banging a sober Sharon was twice as good as banging a drunken Sharon. I'm sure Ready never screwed her. She humped so eagerly, faster and faster, it surprised me. I guess that's where they got the term, banging a chick. I was careful this time. If I got her pregnant, it happened the first time we did it. I was still worried about that first time. We cleaned up a bit and talked for a while. About 11:30, we drove over to the Frosty Freeze on Orange Avenue for a chocolate shake, which we shared with two straws, just like in the movies. Then I drove her home after solemnly promising not to tell what we did.

15

I somehow managed to get through the Sunday LA Times route by eight am and hit the sack.

I called Rich later that day.

"Hey what happened to you last night? We heard Sharon Galloway screaming, then we heard you left with her. I had to drive Larson and Jon home along with Sharon's brother," he said.

"I had another run-in with Stan and Joe Carlson. They tried to shake me down for drug money. Carlson sucker punched me in the kidney but I got Stan good. They were strung out. Then someone threatened to call the cops, so I agreed to meet them outside. They went out the back and Sharon and I bugged out the front. Those two drunken assholes probably waited out back all night. I took Sharon parking in the fog and we hide out from those two. You know I saw that little Mexican Sergio, his father and those two Mexican friends of Carlson's, sitting in a car outside last night. They're pushing drugs everywhere." I said.

"What's this with you and those senior chicks, Mo," Rich said. "Hey, Hampton got laid last night."

"Great, maybe he'll cut down on the booze. Is he gonna to see her again?"

"Yea, I think he's snowed. Now we have another rider with us when we cruise. You can count on her being where Hampton is." Rich said.

"What's her name?"

"Penny something," he said.

We had the week off between Christmas and New Years. That Monday, I decided that since no one would stop this drug stuff at school, I had to do something myself. I paid a dime and rode the ferry over to San Diego. I found the San Diego FBI office near the landing. A young kid like me, I doubted they'd listen. Why even try?

I thought of my amazing neighbor, Boswain Mate Second Class Deacon Morris, and the grit it must have taken for him to struggle to get ahead in the navy. His only way up was to perform an incredible feat in saving two white sailors. They were two men who would never have given him, a black man, the time of day. If I had any balls at all I could at least make an effort to stop the drugs in my school. That's what I told myself. I hated the football coach and Joe Carlson. That's the other reason.

I didn't tell any of the guys what I planned. They'd call it dorky to be a squealer. My thoughts raced with a combination of fear of the unknown, embarrassment, hatred of the coach and Carlson. Would the FBI just laugh at me like the Coronado police? I didn't want to involve my parents. How'd I explain all this stuff? I figured Pop to hit the roof about my allegations and raise hell at school. The school wouldn't do anything. But word would get around. The guys had a point. I'd end up looking like a dork. I hoped to keep my name confidential. Now I didn't even know who to see at the FBI office.

I found the FBI office. Hesitating at the receptionist's desk, I said, "I don't know how you do this, but I want to report some drug dealing."

"That's something for the police, young man." She said.

An older woman with a stern attitude, she sat there with a straight back - no arguing with her. That almost stopped me. About to turn and walk out, I noticed a little gold star pin on her bosom. One last shot. I asked her if she was a gold star mother. That loosened her up.

"Yes, I lost my son in Korea," she said.

"I'm sorry," I said. "My dad served in Korea. He told me that we lost many brave men over there. He taught me to remember them, how hard it was for them, if I ever had something difficult to do." I lied through my teeth. "And to do the right thing. That's why I came to you."

Softening, she took on a grandmotherly tone, "The San Diego police have a very good anti-drug program."

I lowered my voice, looked her in the eye and pleaded, "It's not in San Diego, it's in Coronado. Can't I please just tell someone what I know? There are Mexicans pushing drugs in my school and bribing the football coach to look the other way."

"My, you must be mistaken. I can't see how that would happen at a school. I will get an agent." she said. Then she buzzed inside on the intercom and asked an agent to come out.

A. J. Converse

A man in a blue suit and narrow blue tie came out. He looked at me skeptically and waived me in. He directed me to a cubicle with just a desk, and two chairs. I could see other agents further inside a large open office. Our cubicle's Spartan furnishings, obviously designed for walk in citizens, encouraged a short visit. I explained everything I had seen and heard, including Katie's comment about the Mexican man. After writing a few notes, he introduced himself as Agent VanEp further saying that he'd make a report about it. He was fairly non-committal but did admit that the FBI was interested in drug sales being pushed from Mexico. Then he stood up, extended his hand, ended the meeting, and thanked me for coming in, blah, blah, blah – kinda perfunctory.

From San Diego Bay, the tranquil Southern California sky made the whole thing seem unreal, as if the events that I had just recounted had never happened. Coronado, from the upper deck of the ferry, looked like an insulated little realm, apart from the gritty big city of San Diego and far from the menace of Mexican drug dealers. I wondered if my visit made any difference.

After the Christmas, break a new senior transfer student, arrived at school. Aside from his baby face, something about him looked older. I noticed that after a couple days he sported hard guy Levis and a white t-shirt with a black leather jacket and black dyed huaraches. He buddied up with Del who seemed impressed with him. He looked like a jock. Being a buddy of Del got him into the Stan Huffman group. They all huddled with sandwiches and soda on the patio at lunchtime. From there they'd take off in Stan's car. They probably drove to the beach and smoked pot.

My mind remained occupied. Scared about what to do if Sharon got pregnant, I ran the possible consequences through my mind. If she wanted to keep the baby, that meant I'd have to support it for the rest of my life even if we didn't get married, and shit, we would be expected to get married. There'd be all kinds of pressure to marry. I resolved not to marry her no matter what. Married or not married, I'd still have to support the baby. I couldn't ask my folks to help. Drop out of school and get a job? Shit, none of the alternatives sounded good. The best thing would be for her to give it up for adoption. What if she didn't want to do that? What if she tried to get an abortion? Should I help her pay for it in Tijuana? That was the only place to do it. What if something went wrong? Sharon finally gave me the all clear a few days after the Christmas break. Thank God.

By now, Hampton's new girlfriend hung out with us. She looked bitch'n, with long blond hair and an athletic body. She felt comfortable cruising with us. I guess. She fit in well and stuck with Hampton, but bantered with us like a buddy. Cool. Hampton struck gold with her. She became one of us, a member of the group. We often now cruised in my Buick because it was roomier. Still Rich's car provided transportation sometimes. Penny usually sat on Hampton's lap in the back seat or rode in the middle of the front seat between the driver and Hampton. At parties, Penny and Hampton stuck close. The inevitable happened around the first of April. She got pregnant.

Hampton had to face the things I had worried about. For him it was real. He stopped drinking for a while. His parents and Penny's parents met many times. They ruled out abortion as too dangerous, barbaric and illegal. As Rich said, Hampton may not have been the first of us to lose his virginity, but he was the first to be a father. Penny's parents were upset but reasonable. I understand that the two lovers did the deed one time at her house in her bed. Her old man was at sea and her mom was out drinking wine with some of the officer's wives. Hampton's parents wouldn't let him get married – not in a million years. Hampton and Penny did not intend on getting married anyway. Penny stoically went away to some home for unwed mothers to have her baby and put it up for adoption. Hampton's parents helped pay the bills. The pregnancy affected Penny more than it did us guys or Hampton. He could just go on with his life. Penny endured the ordeal of pregnancy. She moved away. All of us expressed concern to Penny. She had become one of us – well sort of anyway. We were just relieved that it hadn't happened to one of us. It took us awhile before we could enjoy life the same way as before, but soon our memory of Penny faded. Hampton didn't say much about it. He became withdrawn for a while but he got back to his old self after a few months. Penny never came back to school.

By the middle of April, we heard that Jim Nelson had been dropped from the track team. He and Bobby Champ hung out with Stan, Del and Joe Carlson more than ever. The word got around that they were all hooked on something stronger than marijuana. The new guy, Jack Mulligan, bummed around with them.

About the same time, the school fired Coach Adamson - one day there, the next day gone. The rumor went around school that he was caught at the border. He smuggled some guns into Mexico, a strange thing to happen to an Anglo teacher and coach. I figured something else happened that school officials kept quiet.

I continued with my paper route, easier without football. I still put some money away each payday for college, which pleased my pop. That fact helped me several times when I came home with beer on my breath. Plus my good grades of Bs and Cs kept him mellow. The guys and I spent our weekends hanging out at the beach in good weather, or over in Larson's patio drinking soft drinks, bull shitting, and teasing his 12-year-old sister.

Larson lived near Sue Pricey in the newer section of Coronado called the Country Club area. Both their fathers were Captains making Larson cool according to Sue's rules, except he was only a sophomore. She happened to stop over one Saturday in early May with her mom who was visiting Mrs. Bartman. Her last boyfriend had dumped her so her mom dragged her around town to keep her from a deep funk.

Sue entered the patio to chat. Rich and I were peons in her social circles, but Hampton and Larson knew her from some family functions at the North Island O'Club. Her light blond hair and big tits, made up for her big nose. The guys agreed, there may be other hotter looking chicks, but none of us would kick her out of bed.

Since she hung with the big five, she put on a certain manner. Sue thought she was better looking than she really was. That made her confident and direct with guys. Her reputation as fast and clinging had tainted her social standing. She acted unaware of that. Any guy she chased most likely would have to be an officer's kid, or rich or something. She liked to hang out at the Officer's Club pool on the base and entice young officers. They invariably lost interest when they found out her age. That wouldn't be a problem for her later in the year when she turned 18.

She started to gossip about Coach Adamson. She said someone tipped off the Mexican police when he crossed through the San Ysidro border gate. Normally the border guards sleepily propped their arms on the window ledge of the little shed like thing that stood in the road at the gate. They waived each car through without fanfare. It sounded likely that someone tipped them off. She said someone from the FBI interviewed the Mexican transfer student at school after the incident. She said Katie told her the kid was Cholo, a gangster. At that point I remembered Katie told me the same thing.

All this talk about gangsters reminded me that I had talked to an FBI agent about the Mexicans, Coach Adamson, Joe Carlson, and company. It all came together. I realized that the new senior, Jack Mulligan might be a plant. It struck me – they were following up on my tip. I wondered if Sergio De La Puente would be the next to leave school. Did any of the Mexicans know about my role with the FBI? A shiver ran through me.

I tried not to show my unease when I asked Sue. "Is Sergio De La Puente still hanging out with Joe Carlson and Stan Huffman's crowd?"

She eyed me as if she had just realized something. "Oh Hermie, it didn't register that it was you sitting there, you're so quiet. Katie said she sees them hanging out near the Hotel Del Coronado rocks all the time. She can see where they meet from her bedroom window."

"Call me Mo," I said.

125

The guys gave me looks.

"Mo, that's a weird nickname for Herman," she said.

"He got that nickname in junior high school when he got in a lot of fights. A lot of kids tried to call him out, but he always won the fight. I don't remember him starting any of them. It got to be that he was the kid to fight if you wanted to be tough. Whenever some kid started up, he would say *one mo*, that's how he got the nickname, Mo," Larson said.

"Did you ever fight him?"

"No, none of us guys fought him, we were friends."

"Wow, I didn't know all that about you. It explains what I've heard about you handling of Stan and Joe. I guess my friends know that, but we've always called you Hermie because it sounds so cute."

"Yea, I guess so, but my real friends call me Mo," I said.

She leaned forward showing me some tit, I guess in apology for her condescending manner. She was wearing a halter-top that showed a lot already so when she leaned toward me, it was quite revealing. She wore short shorts tight over her nicely shaped hips. My anxiety about the Mexicans dissolved in the heat of my adolescent hormones. I forgot about her nose and started to sense her sexiness. The short shorts were tight in front, which drew my eyes there, and she noticed, but didn't stop talking. Her knees parted slightly. This girl had possibilities. I searched for something to say to keep the moment going.

"So what are those dorks up to?"

She smiled at my choice of words.

"Should I tell them that you call them dorks? Katie thinks they're doing drugs and Sergio is their connection. Joe's Mexican buddies seem to work for him or maybe they work for his father," she said.

"That's bad. Much as I despise Stan and Del, they're gonna ruin their lives doing drugs. I think Carlson is already screwed. But the others, Jim Nelson and Bobby Champ, that's just too bad. And they are dorks. Anyone sucked into that stuff is a dork." I said.

"Jim Nelson dropped out of track because he can't run for shit anymore." Sue said, dropping her uppity patter.

"I know they're trying to hook other kids. They show up at all the parties pushing drugs." I said.

"Well I wouldn't ever touch the stuff myself," Larson said, trying to inject himself into the conversation again.

He had already lost out. Now I had all of Sue's attention. My record of accomplishment in football and kicking Stan's ass apparently impressed her.

"Larson, I'm so impressed. You hang out with Mo and Jon, our two football heroes." Sue said.

That took Larson back a little. He didn't know what to do; either bask in the glory of being buddies with two cool guys, or speak up some more to compete with us. Sue twisted his mind.

"Yea, Coach Adamson sure doesn't choose his players based on how well they play," he said. "Mo and Jon should have played the whole time in each game. Stan isn't much good and Del is hopeless no matter where he plays."

Sue turned and moved closer to me.

"I hope you get to play all the time next year, Mo."

She looked directly into my eyes and her pupils dilated. Things were looking up with this chick.

I lowered my voice. "Will you watch all my games, Sue?" I said.

She giggled.

I glanced at the guys. Larson looked at his little sister when Sue giggled. Rich and Hampton had assumed blank expressions. Jon threw his head back, leaned back in his chair, tucked his thumbs in his pockets, and stretched out his legs looking sullen. I moved closer to Sue.

"My father played football at Annapolis; I've got some old pictures of him at home. You should see the old leather helmets they used."

That sounded like an invitation. Out of the corner of my eye, I saw Rich roll his eyes at Hampton and Larson.

"I'd like to see those," I said.

"You might as well come over now. Mom's taking me shopping later. Once she starts talking, she goes on and on. She can come back and pick me up when she finishes coffee."

"Cool." I said.

A spurt of anticipation rushed through me. I vibrated with readiness, and my head went into a fog. I don't recall exactly how we left the patio. We walked down the block headed to Sue's house.

I felt the pull of attraction between us. Her breathing quickened suggestively, her tits rising with each breath. She brushed them against me as she opened the front door. Then she lead me to the family room, guided me to the couch, and retrieved her old man's Annapolis yearbook from the bookcase. She sat right next to me on the couch, her bare leg pressing against mine. The warmth of her leg stirred my teenage body with adult urges. She leaned against me pointing out the pictures and didn't move away despite my evident physical reaction. I put my arm around her and kissed her.

She kissed back with a demanding tongue and whispered. "Oh God, Hermie, I mean Mo. God I want you, but my parents won't let me go out with an enlisted man's son."

She moved her hand on my thigh. "Doesn't your paper route come near here?"

"Yea," I murmured, moving my hands all over her.

"Ring the doorbell after your route tomorrow. Mom always leaves for church about 7:45, so stop by my house at eight. Check to make sure the car's not here, first." She said.

She seemed so eager, how could I refuse?

I was ready to burst when she pulled away and told me that her mom would be home any minute. She hustled me out the door just as her Mom came up the street. My shirt, worn outside my belt saved me from embarrassment, as I passed her mom on my way back to Larson's.

16

I went home and tried to do some homework, but thoughts of Sue kept intruding. Since I couldn't study, I decided to prepare for Sunday's planned encounter. As I drove my Buick up Orange Avenue to the Rexall Drug Store to buy some rubbers I wondered if minors like me could even buy them. Like cigarettes, did you have to be 18?

With some misgivings, I entered the place and looked at the pharmacy counter in the back of the store. A woman stood there talking to the Pharmacist. Maybe I could just pick a package off the counter and hand it to him without talking. I saw the rubbers in a case behind the Pharmacist – no sign about minors or anything. I sweated it as I waited my turn. When he finished with the lady in front of me, the pharmacist looked at me.

"Yes?"

Trying to keep my voice calm, I said. "I want some Trojans."

He looked at me with a half-smile and said, "What size?"

That floored me. Did they come in sizes?

"Huh?" I said.

"Do you want the box of three, six or a dozen?" He said.

"Dozen."

I hoped I had enough money. I didn't exactly know how much they cost. It turned out I got the dozen for about $3.00. At least after that little ordeal, I knew how to handle buying rubbers in the future. Age didn't matter.

The next morning, I finished my route early so I rode home and dropped off the newspaper bags. Then I slipped in the bathroom, washed all the newspaper ink off my hands, and freshened up. I considered driving my Buick to Sue's house but figured the motor bike would be less conspicuous. I got there about 8:00 am - no family car in the driveway. Again, I was near scoring with one of the big five. What if her mom answers the door? All kinds of crazy thoughts raced through my mind as I walked the motor bike up the stone path to her door and hid it behind some shrubs. I knocked on the door. Sue opened it and made me forget everything but sex. She showed me some things I hadn't tried before.

Sue had to be a nympho. Sue wanted me to stop by each morning when I finished my route. Her mother normally slept late. If her mom ever got up early and found us banging away on the living room carpet, or worse, doing some of the things that Sue wanted to teach me, I dreaded the results. What about the Trojans; at the rate we were using them, I'd be buying a dozen a week at least.

"I don't know...every day?" I mumbled.

She whispered "yes" in a seductive voice.

Pop sometimes said, *if I knew then what I know now...* That's all he said. I wondered what he meant. Now I understood. We decided I would stop by Monday morning.

Then we could decide how often to meet. *Holy shit what did I get into here?* I mapped it out. If I ended my daily route at Sue's house, she could let me in and we could do it on the living room floor while her mother slept in the back bedroom. I told her to be by the front door at 5:30 am ready for my light knock.

I wondered about the effects of banging Sue every which way but Sunday on a daily basis. What would all this cost me? Some of the religion Mom had drummed into me was raising its guilty head. The preachers say fornication is a sin. If that was a sin than what Sue and I were planning would surly send me to hell. Sue sure knew how to fornicate, and how to do everything else that went along with it. I was able to shake off the religion thing, but Sue worried me. I didn't want some kind of personal relationship with a girl like her. She had made it clear that at school, I should simply say "hi" if I saw her. Even her friends wouldn't know. What if she got emotionally attached? She said that she wouldn't, but how would I get out of it, if she did?

Sue said that I better have condoms each time. That was the first time I heard anyone say that word. I knew the word. I read it somewhere but we always called rubbers by the brand name, Trojans. Sue knew all this stuff. I didn't want to catch syphilis or the clap from her. I didn't know much about either, but I heard you could go crazy with syph. How'd I tell my parents if I got a sore down there or something? The thought made me shudder. Adults sure knew how to scare the shit out of horney kids with tales of hell fire and damnation and fears of going crazy and social chastisement. *Hold on, be cool Mo*, I thought. I doubted that an upper class girl like Sue could ever get syphilis, maybe the clap but not syph. *She could have the clap. Naa, doubt it.* Anyway, I had heard clap could be cleared up easily. Plus, the Trojans protected me.

By Monday morning horney again, I put all my fears out of my mind. I finished the route. I parked my motor bike behind the bushes at her house and gently taped on her door. There she was. After 15 minutes of ecstasy, I was on my motor bike headed home. My sweaty body and ink-covered fingers had not bothered her in the least. She was one passionate chick.

This went on every day. Although sexually insatiable, Sue exhibited no special romantic feeling toward me. She just liked the sex and the convenience. Even with the wild sex, the excitement was wearing off. As long as I was banging her, she expected me to stay away from other chicks. Of course, she kept me so satiated; I had little need for other girls. But hell, unless her father transferred or something I might as well be tied to her by my testicles. We kept the affair secret at school. But the arrangement meant I was missing out on other chicks in my social life. Sue was like the *tar baby* in Brier Rabbit - time to break it off.

Larson was the squarest of our bunch, and so far as I knew, the only virgin except for me. Well, there was that time I got to third base that they knew about because they had pretty much broke up a thing at a beach party the summer of our freshman year. Since they ruined my tryst with that chick, they all said it counted for me. Larson sure wanted to end his virginity and join the club. Who better to do it than Sue Pricey? I had to handle the swap deftly because the guys didn't know about my affair and Sue was adamant about not telling anyone. That of course fit into my theory of not kissing and telling. Somehow, I had to get Sue together with Larson.

I walked out of my homeroom one morning headed for my first class, when the principal's secretary came up to me in the hall. She wore a frown as usual, and glasses with a little chain down to a pin on her dress. Her stern manner prevented anyone from daring to question her.

"Herman, please come to the office, Mr. Frenchett would like to see you." She said.

"Huh, yea," I said.

All sorts of things raced through my mind. What if Mrs. Pricey had found out about my trysts with her daughter? Naa, I didn't think the school would get involved with that. What could it be? My mind raced when I stepped into his office. Mr. Frenchett, kind of heavy-set, with dark brown hair receding and turning gray peered out at me through plain glasses. Not imposing, he moved with a certain deliberateness. I doubted he ever took a chance in his life - Mister Square, himself. People in authority always scare me, even Mr. Frenchett, so I stood there quietly. I guess that's the real reason I never caused trouble in school. It wasn't my good character. It was fear - not a very noble reason to stay out of trouble. Mr. Frenchett stood up and ushered me into his conference room.

The conference room had a door to his office and one to the hall. The walls were painted a light cream color. A sturdy looking dark-stained wooden table with a dozen no-nonsense looking wooden chairs of the same color made up the sparse furnishings. The space was well lit, as windows to the street covered one wall. The hall door stood closed. I knew a horde of students filled the hall beyond. Two FBI Agents sat at the table. I recognized one as the agent who had interviewed me in San Diego. I sat down. Mr. Frenchett immediately left the room.

Agent VanEp introduced his supervisor, Mr. Hanson. Both men seemed cut from the same mold; blondish hair cut short in a crew cut, athletic builds. They both wore dark colored suits with white shirts and narrow ties. They said our meeting was confidential and they were investigating very dangerous men. They told me that my previous information helped them tie up some disjointed segments of an ongoing investigation.

They revealed that they had an agent working inside the school. He seemed close to getting evidence on a local drug boss - a Mexican who owned a large farm in Baja. He acted as an intermediary for a gang from Mexico City. His name was Mister De La Puente. The FBI undercover man discovered that Coach Adamson smuggled guns for this group. That's how they caught him.

The Mexicans blackmailed the coach into doing their bidding. The gang set up the affair he had the previous year. The chick who seduced him was a gang member. Once they had him hooked by threatening to expose his affair, they used him to get De La Puente's son into school as a football player. Carlson's friends, the two Mexican hoods, worked for De La Puente. They hooked Joe Carlson on drugs when he visited TJ looking for a prostitute and easy access to liquor. He soon tipped them off to Coach Adamson's corruptibility. It was easy then to get one of the gang's younger prostitutes into Coronado High School. Once in, she seduced the coach outside one of the dances he chaperoned. After he had a number of

136

trysts with her, the gang approached him with the threat to expose him. Then they gradually reeled him in and added him to their payroll. Soon they recruited him to smuggle hard-to-get weapons into Mexico. He had no choice but to do it and each time he did, they paid him, dragging him in deeper.

VanEp said their undercover agent thought the Mexicans suspected him. The agent, they told me, was Jack Mulligan. I had already guessed that. They cautioned me not to play detective, but report immediately if I heard anything on campus about Jack being a cop. They assumed if the Mexicans found out he was FBI, they would kill him. VanEp wrote an unlisted phone number on a blank piece of paper. The FBI always monitored it. He asked me to memorize it, and only call if I heard any gossip that Jack might be an undercover cop.

All that stuff scared me. My initial fear upon entering the principal's office returned in spades. *Shit what had I gotten into here.*

"Don't worry I'm not going to go nosing around. I am a lover, not a fighter," I said.

"We understand you are quite a lover." Agent Hanson said.

Did they know about Sue? Crap.

I put the phone number in my wallet to memorize later. They ended the meeting saying they would stay in the conference room for some time after I left so no one would get any ideas. I didn't want anyone to get any ideas either. They said the principal was to tell anyone asking about them that they were investigating Coach Adamson.

I made it to my first class just as the bell went off. English, I scheduled it in the morning this semester, hoping I'd be more wide-awake. It was such a boring class. Still, I generally tuned out the teacher within twenty minutes. I improved from the previous semester when I tuned out in less than ten minutes. Anyway, most of the grade depended on our written papers not class participation. I tried to say something early in each class to appear interested. Then I tuned out, off somewhere daydreaming. My real problems intervened now - no daydreams today. I started trying to figure out a way to get Larson into Sue's horney clutches so as to extract myself from that situation. My thoughts kept jumping back to the FBI request. That scared me. I hate to be scared. I felt that deep feeling in the pit of my stomach. What was I into here? The situation with Sue floated in the background of my immediate fear.

At 5:30 the next morning, while delivering papers, I got an inspiration and started to develop a plan to extradite myself from the quagmire with Sue and pass her to Larson.

At lunchtime, we all gathered as usual on the patio joking and horsing around. I simply waited for someone to bring up Larson's virginity.

Rich ventured, "So, Larson, when are you gonna get laid?"

"Trouble is, most of the chicks here aren't going to do it unless they really get hung-up on a guy and that takes

138

weeks of dating and going steady. I don't want to go steady. I just want to get laid, no strings attached," he said.

"I think I have an idea Larson," I said.

The guys all looked at me as if a joke or cut-down was coming.

"I think that Sue Pricey is a good prospect for you. Remember that Saturday I went with her to her house. I could really feel her sexiness. She's older, experienced, and now that she doesn't have a boyfriend, I bet she is horney as hell."

"But why Larson," Hampton said.

"He's available, he lives close to her. We just need a way to get her to focus on him and then Larson and her alone. Her hormones will take over. Right now, she just sees him as a little sophomore; we need to get her to see him differently. I don't think she wants a boyfriend right now. She wants to go away to college and find some rich guy or Admiral's son to marry to meet her mom's expectations. But she is one horney chick."

"So why don't you screw her?" Hampton said. His shrewd statement almost derailed my plan.

"I don't want a girl hanging on to me like Penny did to you." A low blow, but I had to get the focus off me.

"I'm trying to get good grades and with my paper route and everything I just can't handle that heavy stuff right now. I'm happy to chase the sophomore girls. But I tell ya,

Sue is the real deal. She is always hot and bothered." I said.

Larson was getting interested.

"So how do I go about getting into her pants?" He said.

"The first thing to do is build up your reputation as a stud in front of the big five. Right now, they just see you as one of the sophomores. They figure you're kind of square. We can start making comments. We can call you studly and imply that you're hung."

"Hey, I am hung." Larson leaned toward us eagerly. I had him hooked. Now I had to sign up the other guys.

"Then we suggest Larson is a bit dangerous. That'll get Sue's interest. Then, once we get her enticed we get them together alone. I'm thinking we might isolate the two of them at a beach party or something."

"I don't know, remember the trouble I got into with Penny. Do ya really want that shit, Larson?" Hampton said.

Jon nudged him. "Come on man, let's do it. Let's get Larson laid. Like you say, it'll be in-fucking-credible."

"In - whale - fucking - hairy balls – Christ - credible, you mean." Hampton was in.

"Okay, so let's do it." Rich said.

So we launched our plan to get our good buddy laid.

That very day after classes, we started. When all the students gathered in groups getting things out of their lockers in the hall, we started referring to Larson as "Mr. Studly." We all went down to Tijuana one Saturday afternoon and got Larson some huaraches, which he died black and started wearing to school. He didn't stop wearing chinos but he replaced the short-sleeve shirts with t-shirts and a vest sweater. We would arrange to have him walk in the center of our group with the rest of us seeming to be trying to keep up on his flanks, especially when walking by the big five. They started to notice him.

Finally, one day an animated Jillian Hankins stopped him as we walked by and said, "Larson why do your friends call you Studly?"

Larson somehow stayed cool and said, "You'll have to ask them."

The big five overheard Hampton mutter under is breath, "Because he's hung."

That was a turning point for Sue. She began joining her mother for tea with Larson's mother. I decided to arrange the next step at a big beach party planned for the first Saturday in May. Sue and I met just about every day after my route. The guys didn't know. She had begun to ask about Larson, so I decided to help things along. I told her that I thought we better stop the morning meetings because her mom was bound to catch us sometime. I told her Larson liked her, maybe she should check him out. That hurt her feelings only slightly, as I had figured. Her obsession with sex had nothing much to do with me. Then she asked pointedly, why we all called Larson "Studly."

After some intentional hemming and hawing, I told her he was heavily endowed. She said she thought that described me. I laughed. I informed her that Larson would be at the beach party Saturday. That seemed to set her mind working, as she was distracted after that, not seeming to notice me as I left.

17

Preparing for anything, Rich and I drove both our cars to the beach party. Larson rode with me. Rich picked up Jon and Hampton. After we arrived, we piled into Rich's car to find a tap. That took about 45 minutes. We got back with a case of beer at 9 o'clock. The party started to rock. A portable radio played *Tequila*. I sat down next to Jill and Sue. Jill had managed to get out of her house by telling her mom that she and Sue were going to a movie. Had they talked about me?

"Hey cool to see you chicks made the scene." Larson said.

Sue greeted Larson with a "Hi Studly."

"Can I talk to you a minute," Jill whispered to me, as we sat down in a semicircle around the two chicks. We walked a short distance from the group.

Jill got right to the point. "Sue and I had a talk. You sure are an active boy. Sue and I are close friends. I've been telling her she shouldn't be so fast. She should get to know a boy first. Just doing it all the time is bad for her reputation. I told her she could get pregnant or catch something nasty like syphilis. Now I hear that you and Sue are having an affair. You're doing it every morning after your paper route. How could you?"

I was surprised Sue had told her. She had sworn me to secrecy.

"How many other people has she told," I said.

"No one so far," she said. Then she repeated, "How could you?"

Pop had told me that women were impossible to figure out. I shook my head trying to understand Jill's logic.

"You made it clear that I couldn't see you again. I don't have a special girl friend. Anyway, she started the affair. So why does it bother you? Did you tell her about us?"

"No, of course not," Jill said. "Sue has some kind of a hang up. She can't help herself. I've told her she should see a psychiatrist. Now she's upset because you're calling off the whole thing. What will she do?"

"What do ya mean, what will she do? It's not like we're in love or anything. She's the one who wanted it that way, just sex. How do you think it's my fault?" I said.

Jill stepped right up to me in that way she has, putting her hands on her hips and whispered, "Well she needs sex, and she doesn't know what she'll do now. She doesn't want to start anything new. The Navy will transfer her father soon. I want to help her, but why do you have to be the one involved. I like you and my friends like you."

The little affair had nothing to do with Jill. What was the big deal?

"That's a lot for me to understand," I said. "I like the sex, but it can't go on forever. Her mom might catch us sometime - what a mess that would be. What do you expect me to do?"

"Just help me figure out what to do," she said.

Realizing that her desire to help her screwed up friend fit right into my plan to hook up Larson and Sue, I told her Larson was the answer. He wanted to get laid badly. I told her to help me put the two together and see if we could get something going. Push a few drinks on them, invite them to walk with us on the beach, and let them take it from there. Jill didn't know she was helping set the trap I had been laying for Sue all along. She said okay. She reminded me our own fling was a one-time thing. Now we were just friends. *Mmm, for 'just friends' she seemed jealous.*

I worried about the little talk I had with the FBI more than rekindling the thing with Jill. I wondered if Stan and company would show up with Joe Carlson and his Mexican buddies along with the FBI's plant, Jack Mulligan.

We walked back to the bonfire. Sue sat close to Larson. Jill sat down next to her and I sat next to Jill. Carlson sauntered up with Stan, Del and Jack. They started making the rounds with some marijuana. The two Mexicans came separately. The local's ignored them as they sat down quietly, smoking marijuana and drinking beer. The Mexicans kept eyeing Mulligan.

Sue cuddled close to an oblivious Larson.

Start making out with her you idiot.

I looked at Larson and motioned with my head for him to kiss her. Square as ever, he ignored me. I needed to get him a little tipsy. I handed him another beer. He took it

145

and drained what was left of the old one, trying to look hip. Sue already finished her beer, so I handed her one of mine. I didn't want her too drunk before Larson caught up. I bummed some rum off a couple of tipsy juniors sitting nearby. I gave it to Larson. I said, "Try this, it tastes great." That got him going.

The Mexicans continued to eye Jack Mulligan. He didn't know the extreme danger he faced. *Crap*. What should I do? Too many things going on, but I had to solve this problem with Sue. I motioned Jill to stand up with me.

"Larson, how about you and Sue take a walk on the beach with us," I said.

Sue answered for both of them, grabbing Larson's hand, "Sure."

It was a cloudless moonless night, with a light fog moving in. We walked along the line of wet sand left by the outgoing tide. Far enough away from the group, where we could see only the light of the bonfire, I stopped and kissed Jill. Surprised at first, she realized the reason. Reluctantly, then a little more eagerly, she played along. Larson finally picked up the cue and kissed Sue, who pressed against him provocatively. We were near the spot where my Buick was parked.

"Let's go up to my car," I said.

We picked our way through the sand, over some low dunes and pickle weed. We finally got to the riprap and climbed gingerly over it to the car. Jill and I got into the front. That left the back seat for Larson and Sue. They didn't hesitate. I sat with my arm around Jill for a few

146

minutes and then checked the rear view mirror. Larson and Sue were lying entwined on the back seat, Sue on top. Bitch'n.

"Jill and I are going for a swim," I said.

Larson mumbled something and Sue just moaned lightly. We got out quietly and walked down to the beach. Jill was quiet for awhile.

"That seems to have worked." Jill said.

"Yea say, lets lie down right here on the beach, Jill."

I was hoping for a repeat of the last time we were together on the beach. She told me to forget it.

18

So that was it. We walked back to the fire. Kids were sprawled about, some drinking, some making out, a rocking party. Jon and a freshman dolly cuddled as Rich whispered earnestly to a sophomore girl. Hampton just sat there drinking. Stan and his crew lounged by the fire smoking marijuana. Jack Mulligan sat with them, but I didn't see Joe Carlson anywhere. The two Mexicans had moved up by the road. I could see them sitting on a concrete bench, drinking beer. That struck me as ominous.

The beer and my success with Larson and Sue made me adventurous. The night got a little cooler. Ignoring the FBI's admonition against playing detective, I zipped up my car coat and sauntered up the boardwalk. Then I climbed up the steps near the concrete bench where the two Mexicans sat. Hidden by the darkness, I snuck behind parked cars to just across the sidewalk from where they sat. I hid behind a car and listened.

They spoke in broken English, but I understood the gist of the conversation. They believed Jack Mulligan was too old to be a student. They thought Stan and his buddies were too naive to have turned in Coach Adamson. Jack was a cop, they concluded. They wanted to report to the boss first. If they got the go-ahead, they would kill Mulligan. Their boss was Sergio De La Puente's old man.

I sensed something. A shadow moved. Something hit me on the side of the head – hard. Barely conscious, I landed on the pavement by the side of the car looking straight at the white-wall tires, which seemed to hold some surreal fascination for me. Then I heard Joe Carlson.

"This jerk was hiding here listening."

Everything got blurry. I felt them lift and throw me into the trunk of a car. It may have been the car I'd been hiding behind. I heard muffled voices as the car started. I tried to pay attention and figure out our direction. My head throbbed. The dark trunk smelled dank. I forced myself to hold down the vomit that wanted to rise in my throat. My mind spun. I let it swim hoping that it would settle down as it recovered better consciousness. Then, I'd think of a way to escape. My heart pounded. The Mexicans were killers. No one on the beach could have seen them take me. They were having too much fun partying. I couldn't expect any help.

After a short drive on what I thought might be Silver Strand, the car pulled on to a bumpy short drive. They opened the trunk and Joe Carlson held a knife at my throat while the other two thugs tied my hands with what seemed to be a bandana. They pulled me out of the trunk scraping my shins in the process. They shoved me to the ground. I winced in pain. They laughed. I feigned more pain and confusion than I actually felt. I hoped for an edge. They had parked off the road behind a small dune covered with pickle weed. I heard a few cars passing. Not much traffic on the strand at 11 pm. I looked at the car, the same nearly new Cadillac that I had seen the old man driving. It had white-walls. He sat in the driver's seat now. Had he been sitting quietly in the car while I was hiding behind it? I bet he made all the life and death decisions.

One of the Mexicans rummaged under the inside of the trunk where the spare tire was stored and brought out a little fold up Army shovel. They talked briefly with the older guy in the car speaking only in Spanish.

Then one said, "Come on Joe, you can help us with this."

They dragged me to my feet and guided me down to the beach. Carlson held me by the arm with his knife at my throat. He said he didn't want to be involved in a killing. He wanted to leave and let the Mexicans handle it.

***

Joe had been headed down to the party from the rest room when he saw Herman Harris sneaking up to the road. He followed him and saw him squat down on the left side of a car to listen to the Mexicans on the bench across the sidewalk. Joe hated Harris even more as he saw him listening in on their conversation. He knew Harris had overheard them talking about killing Mulligan. This was his chance with the Harris kid … to really kick his ass. Maybe they would help him … hold Harris or something … he could really do a number on him … cut him somewhere … maybe cut his face … and threaten to cut his balls off. Now they wanted him to help kill Harris. He didn't want to kill, only maim, he was afraid … he could go to prison … if he just maimed him and scared him, Harris wouldn't tell who did it … but killing Harris … if he were caught …

***

"Hey I don't know about this. The cops will investigate if a kid gets killed." Carlson said.

One of the Mexicans called him a pussy and said there is no killing if there is no body. They wanted him to help dig a grave in the sand down by the high water line before high tide. They told him to dig the grave, then he could take off, but he'd have to walk back to Coronado. That gave me some hope. We were close to the village. The Mexicans, high on beer and marijuana, had tied my hands sloppily. I considered breaking loose and running. They'd just catch me and tie me up better. My heart pounded. My mind raced. I knew that I'd have a better chance running on the beach near the water. I didn't struggle. I decided to wait.

When we got to the area they wanted, one of them came behind me and slugged me with a rock or something. I went down, but was not out. From my old junior high days, I knew how to feign being hurt bad. I let a spasm run through my leg and lay still, my head pounding. They left me there and handed Carlson the shovel. They told him to dig.

"Hey I agreed to help sell drugs, but I didn't agree to this," he said.

"Shut the fuck up or we'll kill you too, you fucking gringo. You do what we tell you now."

Carlson did shut the fuck up. He picked up the shovel and dug quickly.

I lay there a long time and listened to Carlson digging in the soft wet sand next to me. I hadn't been to church in a long time, but I prayed. I promised God that I'd go to church every Sunday with Mom if he saved me from this. It was wet and cold lying there in the sand. My head hurt.

My shins hurt worse. I wiggled my hand a bit and felt the bandanna slip slightly. Then just as I thought I could slip out and just run, Carlson stopped digging.

"It's about half dug. Come on, I wanna get out of here," he said, panting.

The Mexicans just looked at him. One said, "I thought you're a hard guy, one of us. You're acting like a little kid, Joe."

"Yea, yea, but you two can run to Mexico, I have to live here. How can I help you in the drug business if I end up in jail?"

Joe's voice shook.

Finally one said something like, "Bueno, bueno, okay take off."

Then the other said, "Remember, say anything about this and we'll bury you right here too. This ain't no game amigo."

Carlson didn't answer, but I could hear Carlson scurry away from the site, the gutless scumbag.

My murder didn't bother him. His fear of being caught made him bug out on the Mexicans. My growing rage at Carlson seared through my body, overriding the pain and fear. I steeled myself to fight for my life. I'd be damned if I was going to die at age sixteen, murdered by a couple of fuck'n Mexicans. I had to figure out a plan and act before they finished me. Hatred, rage and fear stirred my resolve.

A. J. Converse

One of the Mexicans picked up the shovel and started digging. They wanted the hole deep. I guess the other Mexican lit some Mary Jane. I could smell it. They took turns digging. I could hear them grunt as they tossed shovelfuls of sand. The land breeze blew sand in my face. I lie partially on my side with my face half in the sand. I didn't move. If they thought I was conscious, they would probably finish me right there. They stopped digging after a while. I heard them say something in Spanish. I watched them secretly as they sat down, and lit another marijuana cigarette. The smell made the vomit start to well up in my throat again. I held it down. I opened the one exposed eye hoping they weren't looking my way. Sand covered the other eye. The shovel stayed right where they dropped it. They were sitting on the other side of the grave and smoking, looking out to sea. The little spade was right there alongside the grave and between them and me. Now was my best chance.

I slipped out of the bandana and sprang to my feet, grabbing the shovel in one motion. I hit the closest Mexican flush on the face with the edge of the spade. That put him down before he could react. The other was rising to his feet when I caught him good on top of his head with the flat end. I didn't hesitate. I took off running, carrying the spade.

I ran near the water where the sand was firm, opening up a lot of space on them. I knew that I hurt them. Taking advantage of that edge, I ran hard until out of breath. Then, slowing to a walk to catch my breath, I started up toward the dunes between the beach and the road. When I caught my breath, I started running again. Soon enough I reached the dunes. I slowed and maneuvered around them. As I came around a large dune, I could hear cars passing on the road.

Slipping down to my hands and knees, I peeked around the dune. The Cadillac sat parked down the road about a quarter-mile. It stood in a small depression off the road, not visible to passing cars. The engine was running. The old Mexican was probably still at the wheel. He'd waited for his thugs to do the dirty work. He probably had a gun. I didn't know if the two Mexican toughs had recovered. I figured that if the thugs were not out cold, they would make their way up to the car to tell the old man, then come looking for me.

I spotted the lights from the amphibious base about a mile up the road in the other direction. I jogged toward the base gate, planning to walk up the road to Coronado and then to my car. My experience with the Coronado police didn't encourage me. No point in going to them, I thought. I dreaded getting Dad involved and Mom, she'd have a conniption. I shuddered at the thought of dealing with her. Still trying to figure out what to do, I realized that I had the FBI phone number in my wallet. I knew I must tell them that the undercover guy was next on the Mexican's list.

I dumped the shovel and made my way as quickly as possible along the dunes, stumbling in the dark. My head hurt like hell. Fear drove me on. I heard some sobbing, then I realized it was coming from me. I'd like to say that it was anger and courage that fueled me, but it was plain old fear. I remembered the FBI's admonishment not to play detective. I didn't want to die. I wished I'd never gotten involved in this. Up ahead, I saw a couple sailors leaving the base gate. If I cross here, I thought, I'll be safe.

Then he jumped me. One of the Mexicans had somehow caught up with me. Short but about the same weight as me, he hit me hard, knocking me down. Older, stronger, he straddled me, his hands on my throat. I hit at his gut with my fists. Then I tried pulling his hair and felt a mat of wetness. He must've been the one I hit on top of the head. My hands slipped off his hair. Desperate, I reached down and grabbed his gonads hard and twisted. As a young kid, I amazed my friends and parents by cracking walnuts in my bare hands. I'd put two in one hand and squeeze until one cracked. The other kids couldn't do it. Pop could. Funny what you think of when someone is trying to squeeze the life out of you.

At first, he just tightened his grip on my neck. I remembered the walnuts and squeezed hard and twisted. He had to let go of my neck to try to pull my hand off his nuts. He moaned and kicked. I bent my left leg under me and pushed up flipping us over. I still had hold of his nuts. As he squirmed, I got his body turned and his face pushed into the side of a sand dune. He choked, trying to move his head out of the sand at the same time as he tried to get my hand off his gonads. It took ever bit of my strength to hold him in that position. I sobbed, grunted and willed myself to hold him there. His struggles finally stopped. Thank God.

Puffing, I hustled across the road. If the Mexicans got to the car and back on the road, they wouldn't try to take me in front of witnesses. Some sailors stared at me as I made it across. Now and then cars sped by me along the strand road - no way to tell who was in them. Mostly I just saw their headlights. The thought that maybe I could get help at the gate crossed my mind, but I pictured myself trying to explain what happened to some swabbie. If he called his supervisor, I'd end up with the Coronado police. I doubted they would believe my story, but they might turn me over to pop. He'd be pissed at the situation. Even though I could probably explain it to him, the repercussions would be hell - then, Mom, no telling what she would do. I still had the dumb hope that if I got home all right and did my paper route, everything would be back to normal. That assumed the Mexicans would just go back to Mexico and live happily ever after. *Delusional, Mo.* I decided to walk to my car, then drive to a gas station, and call the FBI number.

I walked on the side of the road. Up ahead and behind me little groups of sailors walked back to the base from their night out. Fortunately, it was dark so the sailors couldn't see my beat up face. I figured the time to be about midnight. My watch had stopped at some point in my struggles. I didn't know where Joe Carlson might be. He could be waiting along the road up ahead somewhere. Scared of involvement in my murder, he probably walked home to hide under the covers like a pussy assed douche bag. *Cool, Mo now you sound like Hampton.* This wasn't over, I knew.

Finally, through blurry eyes, I saw my Buick up ahead along the riprap. Larson and Sue had left it unlocked and probably walked back to the beach party. I started the engine and drove to the nearest gas station. Aching all over, I shambled to the outside phone booth, found a dime in my pocket and dialed.

The woman on the line answered immediately.

"FBI special line, make your report."

I reported my name and said that Agent VanEp had given me the number. I told her all the events of the night, my location, and about the undercover agent.

She said, "We'll have to move fast. I'll make a full report. Go straight home and we'll contact you shortly."

I thought, oh crap, now Mom will be pissed. I figured Pop would calm down once he heard the full story, but Mom, that was something else. Then I thought about my promise to God if I could get away. I realized that no matter how bad the next few hours would be, they were nothing compared to when I lied there, expecting to be murdered. I headed the old Buick toward home.

It must have been 1:00 am or so. Mom was waiting up but Pop was asleep. She looked concerned, then quickly relief showed on her face.

"I had a premonition that something happened to you," she said.

Then she saw my hair and the lump on my head, stood up, and examined it. Concern marked her face again.

"What happened?" She said.

It came out of me like a torrent, what had happened. Pop shuffled into the room.

"What's going on?" He said.

I went through the whole story again. I told them I expected the FBI to arrive shortly.

Pop sputtered about finding those Mexicans himself and cutting their balls off. He said that he'd hold Joe Carlson so I could get in some real licks. About 1:45 am, the doorbell rang.

Pop turned and picked up a vase and headed toward the door saying, "If that's them Mexicans, I 'm gonna bash 'em."

Mr. Hanson and Agent VanEp stood at the door, both sleepy eyed. They had moved fast. They told us that they needed my help once more. After my report, they had tipped off their undercover man. He reported that Carlson, Stan and his buddies planned to meet the Mexicans early Sunday morning to pick up some drugs for sale at school Monday. Hanson said that the gang probably planned to separate Mulligan after the deal so they could kill him somewhere. This was their chance to trap the old Mexican while in the states. They said if he got to Mexico, they'd never be able to extract him.

They told me they needed me to testify against Joe Carlson when the time came. They planned to arrest him and the other guys once Mulligan left with the Mexicans. In the meantime, I was to stay put at home. I told them my papers got delivered at 4:30 am. Pop said to get some sleep, when the papers came, he and Mom would pack them and wake me up when the papers were ready.

Mom and Pop treated me great. I hit the sack at 2:30. They woke me at 5:00. Pop had the car running and they had wrapped and loaded all the Sunday papers in the back seat. I climbed in and Pop drove following my directions. I tossed the papers out the passenger side window. Sometimes I got out of the car to deliver papers to apartments and hard to get front doors. Since we didn't have to make any return trips to load up more papers, we had the route done by 7:00. We got home and I hit the sack again. About 11:00 am, I heard Mom up getting ready to go to church services at noon. I got up, showered, and dressed on time to join her. She said nothing but she patted my hand. Pop was still sleeping when we pulled out of the parking lot and headed to church.

When we got home, Pop was making pancakes. The three of us sat down at the kitchen table and I filled in the details of my ordeal for them. The awful happenings of the night before faded over the warm pancakes, hot coffee and the reality of great parents. I didn't call the guys. I hung around home watching TV with Pop. Around 5:30 pm, it hit the local news. There had been a shoot-out on the Silver Strand near Imperial Beach. Three Mexican drug dealers had been killed.

Agent VanEp called shortly after it hit the news. He told us they had staked out their undercover man and the meeting with the Huffman crowd at the Coronado beach. When Mulligan left with the Mexicans, FBI agents were close behind. Meanwhile a group of Coronado cops busted Stan Huffman, Joe Carlson and some of their friends for possession. The Mexicans took Jack Mulligan to the same area of the beach they had taken me. The FBI moved in before they could shoot him. Mulligan was slightly wounded, but the three Mexicans were killed. VanEp said it was a good thing that De La Puente died. The old man had a lot of influence south of the border. If he had survived and escaped to Mexico, he would never have been caught. He'd eventually get his tentacles back into the US and peddle drugs through other contacts.

19

The next day I did my paper route as usual and drove to school. I met up with the guys at the lockers. The school buzzed with the news that Stan and his buddies had been busted for drugs and the shoot-out on the Strand.

Jon spotted me.

"Hi Mo," he said. "Where did you go Saturday night? Did you know Larson finally got laid? How about that big shoot-out – and Stan and them, what a weekend."

Larson didn't subscribe to my theory that not telling was the best way to ensure a repeat performance. He had already told the guys. News of the drug bust and shoot-out spread all over the school, so kids weren't paying too much attention to Larson. He didn't care. He stood around with a big grin.

Rich said, "We saw you head up to the road. Where did you go?"

I said, "Well I struck out with Jill. Larson and Sue took over my car so I thought I would walk home, then I ran into those Mexicans."

I told them my story. I didn't tell them that I played detective for the FBI. I did tell them that I overheard the Mexicans talking about Jack Mulligan.

Jon said, "Holy shit you're lucky you're alive."

Word got around the school about my escapade with the Mexicans. Gossip about me testifying against Joe Carlson soon got around, making me famous.

"Hey fuzz," some cool-cats said, trying to be hip. Others congratulated me. My stock with the big five hit a new high.

Stan Huffman, Del Webber, Jim Nelson and Bobby Champ all showed up at school dressed in chinos, white socks, black shoes and short-sleeved shirts. Gone were the hard guy Levis and huaraches. They all looked like they had been injected with the fear of God. The word spread that the local police dropped charges. Since Stan had been accepted to Annapolis, the locals gave him and his pseudo thugs another chance. Joe Carlson got out on bail and kicked out of school. Sergio De La Puente never returned to school. He moved back to live with his mother and siblings in Mexico after the local police released him.

Now, whenever I walked by the Huffman goofballs they averted their eyes. The big five girls all started calling me Mo instead of the cutesy "Hermie." Larson was sneaking over to Sue's every morning for a quickie and I was off the hook with her.

With the warmer weather of late spring, the girls at school wore sundresses. In a sundress, Liz Edgerton looked better than ever. I gazed at her now as she walked down the hall toward me. She stood about five-six and wore a bright yellow dress showing some cleavage. She had an impossibly narrow waist and it swelled into perfectly rounded hips, followed by long, slim, well-formed legs. The short dress with a slightly flared skirt revealed a lot of thigh as she walked. She moved quickly toward me at the exit that leads to the patio. Her long black hair rustled gently on her bare shoulders. She carried her lunch bag.

I stood by the exit mesmerized by her walk. It had been a few weeks since I extracted myself from that business with her friend Sue Pricey. Liz stopped suddenly at the door where I stood.

***

Liz was in turmoil. She had heard about what Mo did with Sue. In addition, the other girls seemed to share some secret about him. She still couldn't explain the powerful attraction she had to him since that time she had danced with him. Looking at him objectively, he was just an average boy, perhaps a bit more mature - not handsome, just appealing for some reason. He did it with Sue, Liz was almost jealous. How could she feel this way about a boy that nonchalant about something as serious as sex? Her mom warned her that most high school boys wanted just one thing. They may sincerely believe that they are in love, she had said, but once they get what they want they will dump the girl. They no longer have that strong drive once they succeed because it is based on a primitive need at their age, not love. They simply looked at sex differently than teen girls who saw it romantically. She should be very careful with some boys and keep her feelings under strict control. That's what her mom always said.

When she saw Mo in church with his mother, she had been surprised. That showed another dimension. A boy who didn't try to intimidate other boys, yet clearly respected by them, went to church. Her defenses melted.

BITCH'N

She saw him just ahead. It was as if God had put him there just while she was thinking of him.

***

"Are you waiting for someone, Mo?" She asked.

She alone was talking to me - not just one of the chorus of the big five saying, *Hi Hermie*. In addition, she used my cool nickname instead of the cutesy Hermie that they often used. I looked into her arresting dark blue eyes.

"Huh, no," I answered, like a dork.

I had been headed out to the patio wall where the guys generally met for lunch when I saw her walking toward me. My legs went rubbery, writhing like Jell-O. Liz just had that magic. She got my head spinning, my thoughts swirling. I could handle most girls no matter how pretty, but Liz – cowabunga. I forced myself to act cool, putting my thumbs in my pockets and leaning on one leg.

"Will you have lunch with me?" She asked.

"Lunch? I mean, yes, lunch okay."

I held up my lunch bag to make up for my incoherence. We walked together toward an empty section of the low wall that went around the patio. The guys gawked at me. Trying to be cool, I gave them a little wave and stumbled like a dork. Jon rolled his eyes and I could picture Hampton saying something like "In-fucking-mother-of hairy balls-credible."

Liz's light perfume filled my senses and her slight cleavage captivated my eyes. The breeze blew her dark hair in strands, some of which landed provocatively on her breasts and bare shoulders. I tried to stay nonchalant, but my mind raced to try to find something to say. Her dad was a chaplain and she was supposedly a bit prudish. With her looks, I couldn't see how she could remain that way. And her dress - that was something. A sundress, it was cut low in front. It flared above her knees, showing some beautiful thighs.

***

Liz couldn't explain it. She had impulsively asked him to join her for lunch. What would her friends think? That she wanted to do it with him? What was she thinking? Her mind raced. It felt so nice and comfortable to walk with him, natural like she had done it many times before. She saw him in church. Maybe she could talk about that and God - a good reason to eat lunch with him. She could tell the girls that she had seen him in church. They didn't go to church so much and viewed her as a bit too religious and a bit of a prude. Anyway, they might believe that reason, even though she didn't quite believe it herself.

***

"I like your dress," I said.

She turned to face me as we reached the wall. "Oh thank you, I think the color yellow is cheery, don't you?" She said.

My eyes were drawn to her cleavage, but I dragged them away and looked into her eyes. I got lost in her eyes. It seemed almost an out-of-body experience.

I managed to say, "it's especially cheery on you."

"I saw you with your mother in church Sunday. I didn't know that you went to church." She said.

I hadn't realized that Liz attended the same church. I went to 8:30 am services every Sunday with Mom ever since surviving that run in with the Mexicans. Did God really help me survive being murdered? I remembered praying to him that night. Going to church with Mom was some small acknowledgement that in my mortal life there were things far more profound than I could ever fathom. Maybe He helped me, maybe He didn't, but going to church made me feel peaceful and Mom loved it. Pop had just shrugged.

"I started going again after the two thugs tried to kill me. I used to go with my mom all the time as a kid. My dad never went to church. I stopped going in junior high school. Mom gave up trying to get me to go. But I promised God that if he got me out of that situation I'd start going again." I said.

"Sometimes God is there for us even when we haven't been there for him. I believe that it's because of the prayers of others. Maybe your mom was praying for you." Liz said.

"Mom has always said that she prays at church for my brother and me. I know it was something - I don't know -

something, I felt a presence there that night. Maybe it was God. It kept me going."

"I can tell you've thought a lot about it. You're blessed to have felt his presence. Thank you for revealing that. I wondered why I started to see you in church. I could see you sitting with your mom up in the front because I sing in the choir." She said.

"Mom always insists on sitting in front."

Then Liz started talking about how religion improved her life. She couldn't see why people avoided church. She said that the world would be a better place if everyone went to church. It didn't matter what denomination, as long as they went. I agreed with her. I didn't tell her that I wasn't quite as dedicated a follower of Christ as she because I was mesmerized by her smooth, tan thighs which emerged elegantly from her full, short dress. She talked on earnestly about living a Christian life and loving others as one loves oneself, the golden rule, and all that. I nodded agreeably and noticing the warm glow of the top of her breasts and how her remarkable ass fit snugly on the wall. I admit that I had come to a fear of God during my ordeal, but I still had the urge to sin with Liz, often and recklessly.

It was a beautiful Friday and lunchtime was about to end. We dissected the meaning of life and God's place in it in detail. The bell was about to ring. I took a chance.

"How about I walk you home today and we can talk about this some more?"

"Don't you have a car here?" She said.

"Yes, but it's a beautiful day. I can stash my books in the car and walk you home then come back and get the car after."

"Okay, Mo."

Now I thought I had a chance with this senior girl - one of the big five, here me just a sophomore and the son of an enlisted man. I already had visions of asking her out, kissing her goodnight, taking her to the prom. Whoa, I thought. Don't get snowed.

Yet, at this point, I was hopelessly snowed. I walked back to class, my head full of images of Liz smiling, flirting, laughing, her pretty white teeth, her eyes, her hair, her figure; everything. Jon tapped me on the shoulder and I came back to earth.

He said, "What the fuck's going on? How did you get to eat lunch with Liz Edgerton?"

"She discovered that I go to her church." I said.

Hampton caught up with us and said, "Since when did you start going to church?"

I told him. He said I was running the risk of becoming a square like Larson. Then I mentioned that Larson was banging Sue Pricey all the time now. They agreed that Larson was no longer, what you could call square. He did sometimes go to church, but he went only when his dad and mom dragged him there on some special occasion like Easter. I then told them that I planned to walk Liz home after school. They both stopped in their tracks right there in the hall.

Jon threw his head back and stared at me. "Amazing," he said.

Hampton out did himself. "In-mother-of-humping-fucking-balls-christ-credible."

"I won't tell Liz you said that," I said.

I floated to class and visions of Liz kept me from concentrating the rest of the day.

I met her as she walked out of the gym. Her last class was PE and the girls had been playing field hockey. Still flushed from the activity, she had clearly just showered because some of that long black hair was still wet.

***

She thought about him all day. She told herself it would be nice to have a friend who attended her church. That was the reason, she told herself, that she had approached him. She could talk religion without embarrassment. Other boys teased her about it, but not Mo ... Mo, she had used his nickname. That was how she thought of him she realized ... as more of a man than a boy ... the nickname Hermie that her friends all called him didn't occur to her ... just Mo. But just a sophomore, the girls would wonder about that ... but only a few months younger than her... she would keep him as a friend, not a boyfriend, just a friend who shared her religious convictions ... but she knew deep down that he wasn't that religious, just respectful of her beliefs ... and scared because he had nearly been killed ... how would she have handled those two Mexicans ... she doubted that she'd have fought back ... probably just pleaded for her life ... he was different from the other boys. Then she saw him and her racing thoughts eased, she felt comfortable with him again...

***

"I've got to get some books from my locker," she said.

I had already dumped my books in the car so we walked across the grounds over to the main building to get her books. She started telling me how she had scored a goal by knocking the ball in past that nasty Jennie Talbert. I didn't know much about Jennie Talbert except that she was a muscular junior who kind of threw her weight around, not feminine at all. Then I realized that Liz was a real person not just some idealized member of the big five. I guess I had sort of thought of her as being on a pedestal. I realized then that she had rivals and people she disliked and people who disliked her. A real person, she had no perfume on and her breath smelled faintly of the tuna sandwich she had at lunch. Then I realized that her eyes and her figure still were bitch'n.

We headed toward her home, about eight blocks away in the area of the little cottages with detached garages on an alley that made up the majority of the real estate in the village. Her dad was just a Commander, so the family didn't live in the Country Club area or in one of the smaller houses nearer the beach. We walked quietly; I tried to think of something to talk about. I had just about exhausted my knowledge of God and religion at lunch.

Anyway, I wanted to get more personal, so I could get to know her better.

"You seem to like sports," I said.

"You know, body, mind and soul, they all need to be kept healthy." She said primly.

"Your body sure is healthy," I said.

She gave me a look.

"You play football pretty well. You seem to like sports too." She said.

I didn't tell her my theory that girls flocked to football players.

"Yea, but I'm like you, I believe in studying hard and, aw, the soul."

She caught my hesitation about the soul and smiled a bit.

"So you are not as hip on religion as I am. How come you talked so much about it?"

"Well I told you about my experience with the Mexicans, and aw, well, I figured you like it and I like you..." and my voice trailed off.

She giggled. "You're sweet."

My heart leaped and I almost lost it. Instead, I just grinned at her.

We walked along briskly. She bounced along full of energy letting her hair get tousled in the light ocean breeze. We got to the house. Her younger bother and sister were just getting home too. Unable to ask her to go to the beach with me sometime - the image of her in her bikini flummoxed me - I asked her if I could take her out for a shake or something on Saturday afternoon. It just blurted out of me. I still held her on a pedestal - snowed. Some unconscious part of me must have overcome my awe enough to ask her.

"Sure," she said. "I have to teach some little kids at the church in the morning, so you can pick me up after, say about noon."

***

What happened, she thought ... she had just agreed to a date...letting him walk her home wasn't really a date... but setting a time and everything ... that was a date ... she had said "Sure" ... without even thinking ... she'd never done that before ...she felt so comfortable with him ... yet she felt anxious all the same ... she knew her feelings had a deeper, more primitive base ... her mom had said ... like quicksand ... she had said... but just a date for a shake ... how could that be bad?

***

Wow, I had sort of a date with her now. Play this cool now Herman, I thought. I didn't want to blow it.

I watched her as she walked along the narrow walk on the side of the house.

"Oh, my room is back there," she said motioning at the garage.

Many of the houses in the area had garages with an extra bedroom and bath attached. Some people rented then out to single servicemen. Liz's family used there's as her bedroom. I made note of that as I watched her walk away. I gazed a long minute at her legs and swaying hips in that short yellow dress.

20

Saturday morning I rushed through my route and finished by 5:30 am. I ate some cereal, took a shower and hit my rack until about 10:00. When I woke, I took my Buick out to the parking area, cleaned it with the hose, and dried it off with my chamois cloth. I pulled it near the duplex, grabbed Mom's vacuum, stretched the cord outside and vacuumed the interior and the trunk. I didn't have time to wax it. Then I showered again and put on my best chinos, black shoes, white socks, and a short sleeve blue shirt. I buffed up my shoes with the shoe brush. I drove to the church, arriving at noon on the dot.

Religious school continued to 12:15. It seemed like an eternity. Maybe Liz was standing me up. My heart pounded and crazy thoughts raced through my mind. About 12:15, she opened the door and the kids filed out two-by-two, holding hands to wait for their parents. Most of the parents had already arrived in the parking lot. She saw me, waived, and walked over to my car. A feeling of relief and pleasure washed over me.

She said, "It'll be a few minutes. I have to wait until all the kids are picked up."

She acted very matter of fact and responsible. She looked great in her tight skirt and red sweater. Everything about her was bitch'n. I wondered if she was really as composed as she seemed. I felt like a bowl of Jell-O myself. I grinned.

"Ok, cool."

Finally, the kids were all picked up so she walked over, hopped into the car, and slid over to the middle of the seat next to me. That was the proper thing to do for a girl on a date. A girl only sat on the window side rather than the middle if she was riding with her brother or something. It was wonderful. I put the shift into drive and glanced at her knee, beautiful. It felt comfortable, her body just touching mine. She sat easily with her hands folded in her lap.

"Where are we going for the shake?" She said.

There were two places in Coronado to get a shake, Frosty Freeze where a carhop brought it out to you in your car, or the local Rexall Drugstore.

"Rexall's," I said - "How about a shake with two straws."

She smiled.

***

Again, she felt comfortable with him … just sitting next to him made her feel warm all over … and calm … as if her racing thoughts were okay… she felt his thigh, warm against hers and a sensual feeling began near her hips … she knew what that was … but she didn't move … it felt natural … she had agreed to two straws … that suggested intimacy … somehow she didn't care … she wondered what she'd do if he touched her thigh … while driving …

***

Our heads bumped together sometimes as we sat there, both on the same side of the booth. She told me she was

175

born in Mayport, Florida and lived there until she was about ten and the family moved to Coronado. Her father had been assigned sea duty on a locally based carrier. He had managed to obtain billets around the area since then. That way her family managed to stay in Coronado for several years. She said that currently her father was chaplain on a large cruiser that served as flagship for a group of cruisers. He hoped to get San Diego Naval Base as his final duty station before he retired. She said that he didn't make Captain because there were few Captains in the Chaplain Corps.

"Did you know that I just turned 17?" She said as she wiggled subtly.

"My school in Mayport moved me up from second to third grade. For some reason I was more advanced than the other second graders. That's why I'm just 17 but a graduating senior." She said.

"Just turned 17, huh, I'll be 17 next month. I thought you were 18 going on 19 as a senior," I said.

That meant she was only a few months older than me. *Why did she suddenly tell me that? Maybe she liked me too.*

She went on to say she would have done better on her grades if she had had that extra year she skipped. She got mostly Bs she said. That meant she couldn't apply for the top Ivy League colleges and probably would have to go to school in Southern California. I had no problem with that.

I told her about growing up in Norfolk, Virginia and going to public schools there. I told her how I always tried to get good grades to please Mom and Pop who never had much opportunity, but who were optimistic for their two sons. I admitted that I had stopped going to church in junior high school only after many battles with Mom. Finally, Pop said *for goodness sake give the kid a break.* Mom started going to church alone. I told Liz a little about my fighting and why the guys called me Mo. Then I explained my fear when I was tied up on the beach with those two Mexicans digging my grave.

"Your mom's prayers saved you that night," Liz said.

"Yea, I sure think I had some extra help that night. God, I was scared." I said.

Some of those events flashed through my mind. I shuddered. Then the warm sympathy in Liz's eyes flushed out all those images - those eyes. My gut went back to feeling like a bowl of Jell-O.

We finished our shake. I asked her to take a walk around the Hotel Del's grounds. She agreed. I drove the short distance there and parked by the beach. We walked along the promenade between the hotel and the beach. The swells were coming in rhythmically from the Southwest. All was right with the world. I held her hand. She squeezed it – a great first date - a lot different from my other dates. I drove her home and asked if I could take her out again. I felt like a dork, but what the hell, I was snowed.

***

Something was happening ... she had kept the conversation to their backgrounds and religion ... but he aroused her primitive feelings ... when he took her hand as they walked ... it was so warm in hers ... she just squeezed it ... a sort of a come-on, she realized ... but she couldn't help it. Quicksand, the word kept popping into her mind ... was this what her mom meant? ... Mo wasn't like other boys was he? She knew that she wanted to see him again ... and again ...

***

She hopped out of the car, ran around to my side, kissed me on the lips, and said, "Call me."

21

Her parents wouldn't let her go out on school nights, but I saw Liz Friday night, Saturday and Sunday for the next two weeks. I saw the guys only during the school day. Although I missed the weekend escapades with the guys, Liz had my attention all day and all night. I couldn't get my mind off her.

Liz and I didn't do much in the sex department. She let me kiss her, but I was always restricted to above the neck and hugging her. It didn't matter, I was still as smitten as ever. I did manage to French kiss her. Once she tried French kissing, she loved it. I had put Joe Carlson out of my mind. Stan and his crowd had reformed. They were suddenly square as could be. With Liz in my life, the incident on the beach with the Mexicans, the FBI shootout, and my agreement to testify against Carlson faded from prominence in my consciousness.

I decided to ask her to the prom. I sweated that more than having to testify against Carlson. What if she said no? I'm only a sophomore. What if she tired of me? What if she didn't like the French kissing? What if she felt I took things too slow? No, no she held me back. I wanted to get more intimate with her. That would make us closer. Closer - that kinda scared me. *Holy shit how did I get so screwed up over a chick?*

I finally asked her at the end of one of our Sunday milk shake dates. She beamed and said she'd love to go. She would ask her mom and dad first, because they'd have to buy her a new dress, and they'd have questions about after-parties. But she was sure she could go.

Bitch'n.

I knew there were many house parties after the prom. Some kids rented hotel rooms so they could change clothes before going to the after-parties. The prom committee scheduled the prom breakfast from 6 am to 9 am at the hotel. Some kids said that they planned to go to the after-parties and then the breakfast. Willing parents said okay for this was a once-in a-lifetime thing. Some couples planned to shack up in the hotel instead of using it for changing for the after parties. For many who went, the prom was a one-time thing. All sorts of chicanery and hoodwinking of parents went on. Of course, the parents knew all the various things that could happen at prom, but they believed that other kids did those things, not their own kids. I wasn't sure if Liz's parents would allow any after-parties. I figured her parents would want her home promptly after the prom. I was prepared for a platonic date on prom night.

I met with the guys at lunch on a Wednesday in the middle of May. Jon said what was on all their minds.

"So, you too uppity to cruise with us lately, Mo," he said.

"Sorry guys I've been dating Liz Edgerton."

"What are you in love or something?" Jon pressed.

"No, no, well snowed, I guess," I said. My face reddened.

"Hampton brought Penny along with us when we cruised. What are you doing with Liz that's so private? You screwing her?"

180

"No, no nothing like that. Look, how about instead of just meeting Liz for lunch today, I bring her over here or, maybe you guys can ease over by the big five. I'll get Liz to sit with us. What's the deal with you and Sue, Larson?" I changed the subject and I knew Larson was busting to talk about his conquest.

"I'm taking Sue to the prom," he said.

Then he lowered his voice, "I haven't told anyone but you guys about Sue and me. She set me straight on that. Loose lips sink ships, she said, or something like that."

"More like loose lips stop heaving hips," Hampton was back on form.

"Anyway, the big five think Sue asked me to take her to the prom as a friend so she wouldn't miss the experience of a lifetime." Larson said.

I didn't think that the big five believed that. Jill helped me set them up and she participated in the scheme, so she surely knew the truth.

I saw Liz waiting for me over by the girls. I waived and walked over.

"If you don't mind eating with my friends, maybe they'll come over here." I said to Liz so that the other girls could hear.

"Sure, they can come over."

All five giggled.

I waived the guys over. We found out that Sharon, Katie and Jill had no dates for the prom. They had no steadies and apparently, the other senior guys hesitated afraid to ask these upper crust chicks. Their high requirements made them unapproachable. Some seniors were taking junior and sophomore girls instead.

"Why don't we all go together and get a table and sit together. The three girls without dates can go with the three guys without dates and we can all be one happy group." I said.

"You're a genius," Rich said.

"Why would we want to go with a bunch of sophomores?" Jill said.

"Because we're cool," Rich said.

"And that car of yours is a piece of junk." Jill said.

"I promise to wax it and vacuum it just for you." Rich said.

Rich and Jill bantered back and forth.

Finally, Katie said, "I think it will be okay as long as we go as *just friends.*"

So we agreed, and we hadn't even decided which of the three girls would go with which of the three guys. That could be worked out later. I didn't want this arrangement to fall apart so I suggested we check our funds, go ahead, and buy tickets. The prom committee set up a little table on the patio to sell tickets. The ten of us all approached

182

the table laughing and the guys bought the tickets. We reserved a table for the whole group. Coincidently the Hotel Del Coronado, which was hosting the prom, used tables set for ten people. The prom was scheduled at the hotel for Saturday, June 6 - in two weeks.

The next day at lunch, we sat with the big five. Larson and Sue were careful not to sit next to each other. I sat on the edge of my group next to Liz who sat at the edge of her group. I brought up the question of after parties and breakfast to Liz. She said that her parents had tentatively approved the after parties and breakfast but they wanted to know the details. I suggested that the girls rent a room in the hotel for changing. I figured parents' minds to be more at ease with the parties if they knew the girls were going together and changing together. The girls agreed to talk about it. Liz would get back to me.

Later, I saw Jon and told him about the plan for the after-parties.

"That's a good idea," he said. "Maybe we can use the room to change, too. We can chip in half the money."

"Yea," I said, "but that better not get back to the girls' parents."

"So how do we split up the three girls?"

"Hampton fits good with Sharon. His old man being a Captain will impress her parents. I know Jill appreciates Rich's dry sense of humor. You and Katie work because both your parents have money and aren't military."

"Katie, huh, she is one hot chick," he said.

He was hooked. I enlisted him to help me line up the other two guys, not that they'd need much persuading. Liz would have to sway the girls. That wouldn't be hard either. Now I just had to figure out how we could all go with just two cars among us. With all this stuff to arrange, I completely forgot about Joe Carlson and the night I spent on the Silver Strand waiting for my grave to be dug.

By the end of the week, everything was set. The girls agreed to the individual date match-ups. Larson informed us he and Sue would use his family car. While we all basked in the sun on the beach that Saturday morning, Hampton summed it up.

"It was completely mother-fucking, whale-humping, mother-of-hairy-balls, in-fucking-duck-christ-credible."

"Creative, man," I said.

Rich added, "bitch'n."

I left the guys to meet Liz after her religion class.

After the kids were picked up at the church, Liz popped into my car and started talking excitedly about college. She had been accepted to the University of San Diego, an elite Catholic college. She decided to live in a dorm and study liberal arts. After her four-year degree, she hoped to get a teaching credential.

I didn't care what she planned to study, she'd be close by.

"What about me?" I said.

184

"Oh we can still see each other sometimes, Hermie." She said.

She used the cutesy name I hated. The girls liked to use it when they felt affectionate in a big sister way toward me. She saw me wince and immediately corrected herself saying, "Oh I mean Mo."

That simple statement deflated all my fantasies of a golden future with Liz. I was too snowed to understand the facts, just a 16-year-old high school kid dating my 17-year-old crush. Many things would come between us in the future.

I took her to Rexall's Drug Store fountain for a chocolate shake. We took a booth. She talked incessantly. When she realized I sat there next to her, she'd interrupt her babbling to tell me we would still be *great friends* in the future. However, her excitement about college eclipsed any feelings toward me. Only the little glimpses I got of the swelling of her breasts kept me attentive. At least she felt close enough to share her dreams with me, but friends?

***

Liz's mind raced again ... had she discouraged Mo. Oh she didn't want to do that ... she tormented herself about going further with him or losing him ... or discouraging him ... and all that babble about college ... what so excited her about that - she wouldn't be moving away... they could see each other ... but instead of that she had babbled on and on about the college itself ... and lately their dates ... she loved French kissing but her body wanted more ... after their dates she buzzed for hours ...

she couldn't get him off her mind. Her mom always told her about this quicksand.

***

I dropped her off, collected a nice kiss and drove home. I found Mr. Hansen and Agent VanEp sitting with my parents at the kitchen table drinking coffee. Their faces were serious.

"It looks like things are coming to a head," VanEp said.

All that business came back into focus like one of those cartoon anvils dropping out of the sky on Road Runner. Planning for the prom and dates with Liz helped me put it out of my mind. The distress on my face must have registered on Pop. He patted me on the back.

"We're proud of you son," he said.

I looked over at Mom, saw her smile, and nod agreement. The agents went on to explain that Joe Carlson's first hearing came up shortly. First, the judge would determine if the FBI had a case, then Carlson would make a plea and choose either a jury trial or trial in front of a judge. Carlson could accept a plea bargain. They already offered him three years in prison and then probation for a guilty plea as an accessory to attempted murder. His old man the Colonel, said no to that. The Colonel believed his son was coerced to help the Mexicans. Carlson was over 18. The FBI planned to offer the plea to him again without the Colonel being present.

They went on to say, the fact that Joe had chickened out at the last minute didn't change the fact that he helped arrange the attempted killing. He hit me on the head, after all. If Carlson hadn't been such an asshole, I might have sympathized with him. Wasted on weed and God knows what else, his didn't resist the Mexicans - a pitiful case. He was an asshole. Now I just didn't care what happened to him. I wanted to get the whole thing over quickly.

22

By Tuesday of the following week, the girls' parents agreed to foot the bill to rent a room at the hotel prom night. The girls decided that the boys could use the room for changing. Each group would change separately. Since the girls didn't want their parents to know about the boys using the room, the boys got out of paying. Anyway, the guys paid for the tickets, corsages and rented tuxedos. Liz and I decided to drive Jon and Katie. Jill and Rich agreed to drive Hampton and Sharon. We all informed our parents that we would be changing in the hotel room. The girls' parents never double-checked with our parents. Bitch'n.

I heard that Stan and Del asked some junior chicks. I guess they impressed them with their "studly-hood" or something.

I spent the rest of the week studying or doing my paper route. Finals were coming up. Conscientious enough to try to raise my Bs and Cs to all Bs I hit the books hard. I did take some time out to rent a tuxedo with a powder-blue jacket that the rental shop promised was the "in" thing. I bought a corsage with help from Mom.

Saturday morning the guys hit the beach. I got there after my paper route. The beautiful spring day made the water sparkle. We surfed all morning without the chicks to distract us. In fact, few people were on the beach. When we did take a break on the sand, we speculated about the coming summer and the prospects of seeing the current crop of high school girls in their bikinis on the beach. Who

A. J. Converse

would replace the big five as the queens of the Coronado sands?

We plotted our moves at the prom. We decided to use the hotel room for making out, if the girls agree. Maybe if we showed them a great time, they'd be up for some necking. Larson said if we used the room for that, he and Sue would use his car. We knew what he planned. I told the guys Liz probably would resist using the room for necking. She would call it the "near occasion of sin." I got a lot of snickers for saying that.

Mom had spaghetti for dinner. I ate lightly and stayed away from the garlicky meatballs. I showered very carefully and brushed my teeth repeatedly. I used some of Mom's Listerine mouthwash. I was really slicked up for the event. I left the house at 7:00 to pick up Liz.

When I rang the bell, her mom answered the door. She told me Liz needed more time to get ready. She invited me in. The small living room looked about the size of my parent's living room. The stylish furniture made the room seem larger. The place practically sparkled. The two younger kids sat there pretending to watch TV. They eyed me. Liz's dad asked me about school. I told him I took college prep courses. That seemed to satisfy him. Liz's mother was hovering about with her Pentax camera.

Liz finally appeared, wearing a dark pink strapless chiffon dress. She looked bitch'n. I knew her old man noticed my glance at her partially bare breasts, delightfully framed by the dress. I stared, holding the corsage in a box in my hand.

Her mom said, "Go ahead and pin it on, Herman."

BITCH'N

***

The prom ... her mom was excited about it all day ... hustling around ... altering Liz's dress here and there .... Liz was nervous too ... she had decided ... sex with Mo tonight ... if he wanted ... what if he declined ... she hoped he wouldn't, then she hoped he would ... she didn't know ... did that mean she'd never see him again ... if she did it? She tried to appear calm ... he looked so good standing there with the corsage ... cute ... standing there ... would he touch her to pin it on? ...

***

I looked at her – my pulse went up. I took the corsage out of the box and Liz came close. I tried to figure out how to pin it to her left chest without actually touching the bare skin of her breast. She stood calmly in front of me, her eyes directed at mine. I stood there like a dork.

Finally, her mom took it from me and said, "Here I'll do it."

She tied it to her wrist. Then there were the pictures. Liz's mom insisted on pictures of the two of us. Then she had me snap some pictures of Liz with her dad, then with her, then with both of them. Finally, I found myself taking a picture of the whole family.

As we left, her sympathetic father said to me, "Well you made it through that, Herman. I bet it was tougher than making a tackle on the football field."

I had to agree with him.

Quiet, Liz squeezed my hand as we headed out to the car. She looked beautiful sitting there. She slid over next to me. I glanced down at her cleavage about a hundred times, I guess. We drove by Jon's and picked him up. His mom actually waived at him and us from the porch. He held a bag of something in his hand besides Katie's corsage in a box under his arm. After we pulled away from his house, he pulled out a bottle of rum that his brother had bought for him.

"Rum and cokes tonight," he said.

We got to Katie's mansion, which impressed Jon. His mom's house was ritzy but nothing compared to Katie's. He left his bag in the back seat and nearly skipped to the door.

"You're quiet tonight Liz. Are you nervous?" I said.

"I'm a little nervous, but sad, mostly."

"You know that talk we had at the Rexall Store Saturday; well my parents had a little talk with me and they don't want me to see you after the prom. They just think I have spent too much time with you lately and want me to concentrate on college instead. They said that boys can wait until I am a little older," she said.

"But you told me you just wanted to be friends."

"Yes, but I want us to see each other again."

"So you like me more than you let me believe," I said.

"Well, yes, no, oh Hermie, I don't know. But I don't want you cut out of my life."

"Wow, thank you for telling me that." I said. "I thought you wanted to drop me and let me off easily."

Then Jon came out as jaunty as can be with Katie on his arm. I had to admit, Katie still was stunning and the two looked good together. My mind raced from that night with Katie, a little jealousy about Jon and her, to Liz and euphoria about her admission. What a night of revelations.

Jon interrupted my thoughts by asking if we minded having the rum at our table. He wanted to sneak it in to mix with our cokes.

Liz said, "I'm all for some real drinks tonight."

"Count me in." I said.

Katie said, "Oh, cool."

Clearly, Liz and I had a lot to talk about. I found her hand in her lap and squeezed it. She looked at me and smiled. We parked and got out to walk into the great ballroom they call the Crown Room. Rich, Jill, Hampton and Sharon sat drinking cokes at our table. Jon had hid the rum bottle in Katie's purse. He hustled Katie ahead so he could tell everyone about his coup, the bottle of rum. A few minutes later Sue and Larson arrived. Sue looked a bit rumpled. A quickie before the prom, I thought.

I shook my head at Larson who grinned broadly. We all ordered cokes and passed our glasses to Jon who sat with his back to a wall. The long white tablecloth reached down to the floor and provided a perfect cover. He turned the cokes into Cuba Libra's quickly. He put a little extra rum in the girls' glasses. The noise picked up in the room as the band started playing. It was impossible to hear.

Across the room, Stan and Del along with Jim Nelson and Bobby Champ sat with their dates. They looked as square as could be. One would never realize that they had been the town's hoods. Of course, Joe Carlson was probably at home under the eye of his old man - out on bail, but restricted to his home.

I danced with Liz who acted like Miss Proper in the way she let me hold her. I found the formal pose cool. At about 10 o'clock the girls opted out of a break for pictures since they were with a bunch of sophomores. They said it wasn't us. It was just pictures for seniors. Then I noticed Del and Stan getting their pictures taken with their junior dates. I stayed cool.

***

Her thoughts raced again ... thinking about the rest of the night ... she had decided to tell Mo to wait with her after the girls changed ... she would say she had to use the restroom, then when the others had gone to the first party she would come out and they could use the room ... every time she thought she might lose him if she did it ... or she might lose him if she went away to school ... or her parents would step in ... or anything that would break them up... she squeezed his hand... that's all she could do ... for now.

***

BITCH'N

Liz kept squeezing my hand for some reason. I asked her
to walk outside for some air. She agreed quickly.

"The way I see it, we both want to see each other in the
future, so we should regardless of what your parents say."
I said.

"Yes, but they'll have a lot to say about where I go this
summer, and they want me in a dorm at USD in the fall so
it will be difficult," she said.

"Let's try to make tonight something memorable in case
we can't see each other again for awhile." I said.

"And what do you mean by that kind sir?" she answered
with a smile.

Then she said, "Let's have - some more rum and coke
and see what happens."

She slurred her words when she said that. We were both
getting high.

I kissed her then and she kissed back, hard. We went
back inside. We had a couple more drinks before the
band played the last dance, a dreamy version of *Twilight
Time*. While we danced, it was clear that she had made a
decision. She whispered that after we all changed into our
after-prom clothes, we could stay around the room for a
while after the others left. She told me that when the
others were ready to leave she would have to use the
bathroom. I could stay and wait for her. We'd tell the
others that we'd see them at the party. I didn't argue with
that.

194

When the dance was over, we went back to the cars and the girls retrieved their after-party clothes. The guys then waited in the lobby while the girls changed. We changed after that.

While we sat in the lobby, Rich said, "Larson, did you and Sue do it in your old man's car before you got here?"

Larson grinned and said, "She's hard to keep up with."

I remembered when I had a strong desire for Katie, so I asked Jon how things were going.

He said, "She seems to like me but she stressed that she is a senior and that there will be no more dates after tonight. She has a thing that her parents want her to stay away from Anglo boys as much as possible. But I'm hoping for a good make-out session later."

"Uh huh," I said.

After about a half-hour, the girls came down and gave us the room key so we could change. We went up to the room. Rich immediately headed for the closet to check out the girls dresses. He said he wanted to figure out what held up Jill's strapless gown. I don't know what he found out. We changed and hung the rented tuxedos in the closet.

True to her word, when we met the girls, Liz said she had to make a trip to the ladies room and for me to wait for her. The others said they would go ahead. Since one of the first after-parties was at a large house near the hotel, they decided to walk and leave the cars in the parking lot.

***

She knew it was going to happen now ... a heady feeling ... like she felt carried along in a rip tide ... dangerous ... sensuous ... churning ... she was sinking into the quicksand ... desire ... the work of the devil ... how could something so good be the work of the devil... she felt eager to get Mo back up to the room ...

***

Liz and I went back to the room. A small lamp on a bedside table lit the quiet room. The anticipation between us felt tangible. She fidgeted. I knew she was upset by her parent's edict. I figured that she was nervous about having sex for the first time. Liz gazed at me steadily. She asked me to turn off the light as she fidgeted with her blouse. I helped her unbutton. We fumbled around because of her inexperience and my desire to treat her like a princess. Our cloths came off, then it got passionate. The beauty of it stunned me. It was a far deeper experience then my other trysts. Was it love? That word scared me, but Liz, being with her, made everything all right. After, we just laid there for a while.

She told me she never had sex or even went to second base before, because of her religious background. Her feelings for me sorely tested her religious beliefs. Her parents' restrictions intensified her feelings. If her parents had allowed her to continue to see me, she probably would have resisted her desires longer.

"I'm glad we did it. I am glad it happened the first time with you. It felt beautiful," she said.

"Now that we know how to do it, we can practice a lot and you'll like it more and more." I said.

She giggled.

"We need to make the best of any time we have together. My parents think that I care too much about you. I love my parents. I don't want to hurt them, but I don't want to lose you." She said.

"We can still care about each other and see what develops and I do care about you. Do you really care *too much* about me?" I said.

"Yes."

That was as close as we got to using the L word.

23

It was now about 2:00 in the morning. The others had been gone for about a half-hour. Liz asked me to go and get us each a coke or something. I headed downstairs to get cokes at the bar. I found the bar closed and the hotel lobby quiet. I remembered seeing a soda machine near the parking lot when we came in. I walked outside into the balmy air, headed toward the coke machine near the hotel on the side of the pool. I saw a shadowy figure in the parking area. I figured one of the guests got back late. I turned to the vending machine and put in a quarter. I truly believed then that God existed. Liz and I were part of his design...

***

Joe had climbed out the bedroom window. At first his enforced restriction to his house had been okay. He felt better than he had felt in a long time. Hell, he didn't even remember half the stuff he did the night they said that he and his Mexican friends tried to kill Harris. His old man spent more time with him and Loretta had stopped bugging him. When the voice came back, he tried drinking his old man's liquor. The Colonel discovered him pilfering it one night and locked the liquor cabinet. It wasn't much help anyway. Only weed kept the voice away. Now it tormented him again. A couple days before, the voice had become nearly a constant drumming on his brain. He alone heard the voice. It sounded like Herman Harris. With no weed to stop the voice, he must kill Harris to stop it. The prom was tonight; maybe Harris was there.

***

As the bottle came out, a shape moved to my right. I looked. Carlson stood holding a knife. He made a noise like kitten's meow and came at me. Some primitive reflex in me dodged his lunging hand. I swung the bottle at his head, hitting a glancing blow. Only then did my brain register what had happened. I took off running hoping to reach the lobby and get help. He moved faster and tackled me with a frenzy. Kicking, squirming, I eluded the slashes.

"I'm gonna fuckin' kill you!" he shrieked.

His pure hatred brought the prospect of death, the end of everything, Liz... everything.

With blood shot eyes, he grabbed at me in a crazy frenzy. I staggered away toward the pool. He blocked the way to the lobby. I ran my heart on fire with fear. He groaned and snorted behind me. I couldn't outrun him in his half-crazy state. His high-pitched wail boosted my terror as he chased me. Blood dripped from his cheek where the bottle had hit him. I felt his desperation. It was tangible. I knew he must kill me.

At that instant, I saw myself in him and he became a fiend. The same primitive part of him existed in me, the primitive part that could kill. My terror turned into that same bestial anger. All my senses heightened, I felt the presence of God. My mind leaped out of my body. It watched everything. A sudden confidence filled me. Somehow, it would turn out all right.

BITCH'N

Ahead, like an omen from God, stood a stand-up ashtray, heavy, with a weighted, rounded bottom. The fiend closed to only a few feet behind me, stumbling and swearing, giving no quarter. I could hear his unnatural noises. I watched some primitive part of me surge to the surface. It took over like a rip, a churning current of anger and hate. I grasped the ashtray with unholy strength. I swung it hard at his face.

Down, the fiend still clutched the knife, his arm quivered spastically. It hurt him bad. Hatred swamped me. Like some apparition, I looked down on myself. I could see myself kneeling, holding his shaking hand and squeezing it in an unbreakable grip. I seized his other hand and stabbed it with the hand holding the knife. One slash finished it. The knife plunged deep into his wrist. I leaped back as a pulsing stream of blood squirted out of the wound. I stood up quickly, panting.

The demon evaporated. God was gone. I again occupied my body. I looked around.

No blood splatter on me. Carlson lie semi-conscious, his hand still gripping the knife stuck in his wrist. He shuddered as if in a fit or something. I realized he would die with no medical help.

Fuck him.

I walked away trying to catch my breath. I walked back to the vending machine, picked up the bottle I had hit Carlson with and bought another coke. I stopped in the lobby's public rest room to get my wits back. Panting, I checked myself out in the mirror. Briefly, it seemed as if I looked into a broken mirror. My face appeared distorted.

A. J. Converse

A second Mo seemed to hover half out of my body so that there were two Mos half together and yet half apart like a view through binoculars that need focusing - fuzzy. I brushed off my chinos, washed my hands and looked again. I appeared normal; just one Mo stared back at me. I didn't look like someone who had just stabbed a kid, probably to death. I washed the coke bottle that had hit Carlson.

A single clerk dozed at the front desk in the quiet lobby. My mind had been in some terrible place. I saw everything so clearly now. The terrible place faded. I composed myself. I couldn't report it. It would scare the hell out of Liz and then she would avoid me. Her parents would forbid her from seeing me. No matter how I explained what happened, she would be lost to me forever. I could claim self-defense; the authorities might believe me, maybe. I knew when I had stopped defending myself and when I had simply murdered Joe Carlson. He couldn't survive with all that blood pumping out of his wrist. No one needed to know of my overwhelming hatred. They didn't need to know that about me. No one could know.

My mind strangely clear, I took the elevator up to the room. The sight of Liz waiting for me in bed made me forgot everything. She looked so beautiful. We made love wildly. It was as if she knew what had happened to me. The same demon of primitive frenzy possessed her. It wasn't real, the demon. Yet even Mom always said the devil really exists. I had felt God on the beach that night the Mexicans tried to murder me and again tonight. The demon appeared tonight too. Was this murder an act of the devil? Where was God when I killed Joe Carlson? Liz and I existed apart from God and the devil. Shaking my head, I thought, *What the hell.* We drank our cokes.

About 3 am, the other couples stumbled back. They found Liz and me sitting there in our after-party clothes talking. They gave us puzzled looks. Crocked on the rum and whatever else they drank at the party, they came back to neck until the next one. We joined them like good high school kids. It was fun. Liz giggled as we kissed and watched the others. The girls had apparently decided a little necking with sophomore boys wasn't going to get them kicked out of the senior class. Of course, Sue and Larson went into the bathroom and locked the door. Later, in a great mood we headed for the last after-party before the big breakfast.

I felt like a split personality. Here I was at prom with a great girl and some good friends and getting a little wasted. An image I tried to suppress, kept popping up in my mind of Joe Carlson's wrist spouting blood like a pump.

We got to the next after party. It consisted of a keg of beer and music from 45s stacked on the record player. *Splish Splash* played loudly. Some couples danced slowly to it. Others bopped. Couples huddled in the corners making out. I poured Liz and me each a large size cup full of beer from the keg. I drank mine quickly and then had another. Liz looked at me funny but didn't say anything. By 6 am, I felt high, with a headache coming on.

We all walked back to the hotel for the breakfast. Most people dragged. I felt a bad hang over waiting to hammer me. I still had my paper route to do, *God*. Liz and I ate pancakes and drank coffee. I picked up a couple of mint candies as we left for home. We both munched them.

"You're quiet. Do you regret it? Will you forget me?" She said.

"No, no," I said. "It's just that I'm tired and have a hang over. I won't forget you."

"Well, I don't regret it, even if you do. I know some boys lose interest or something once they get what they want," she said.

She didn't have a clue of what I had on my mind. That spouting blood from Joe Carlson's wrist played like a newsreel in my head, again and again.

"Liz you're a dream girl, I'll never forget you. But you told me I have to back off because of your parents." I said.

"I know, I know, I'm confused. You confuse me."

Then she smiled a beautiful smile. How could I resist that? I kissed her. Then we got into the car. She slid comfortably over next to me. She said not to call her, instead I could meet her after her religion class on Saturday and we could go for a chocolate shake.

"Can I send you roses?" I said.

"God, no."

I walked her to the door at 6:30 am. She carried her prom dress on a hanger that her mom took out of her hand as she arrived at the front door. Then Liz gave me a nice kiss in front of her mom. I drove home.

My papers sat folded on the front porch. Good old Mom and Pop had folded and stuffed my newspapers for my route. Pop was up, sitting at our little kitchen table reading the paper and drinking coffee. Mom had gone back to bed. He said he would drive me around the route. I hadn't planned how to handle my route. Mom and Pop had covered for me again.

I changed out of the tux while Pop loaded my car with papers. He handed me a big mug of coffee when I came out to the car. We chatted quietly as we covered the route. He enjoyed hearing about the evening. Of course, my tale left out my success with Liz and the Joe Carlson attack. Telling him what I knew he wanted to hear, I said that drinking wasn't such a cool thing. It gave me a headache and made me feel blah. He probably didn't believe a word I said about not liking the effects of drinking. By eight o'clock, we headed home. He suggested I take three or four aspirins and hit the sack.

As we pulled in, I noticed the FBI car parked near our unit and my heart pounded a bit faster. Fortunately, my hangover made my responses lethargic and kept my heart rate slow. Still, a deep dread started in the pit of my stomach and filled me like a spreading pool of blood. We walked in. Mr. Hansen and Agent VanEp sat at the kitchen table drinking coffee with Mom.

I stumbled a bit entering the kitchen. I attempted to keep my face blank. It must have registered some apprehension even as fatigue and the after effects of the drinking kept my thoughts operating in slow motion. Every detail of the moment entered some deep unconscious part of my mind. The tiny drop of coffee next to VanEp's cup, the sprinkling of sugar near the sugar bowl, the dripping faucet in the sink, all these little things my mind examined. It was as if some part of me tried to avoid the looming questions to come and looking desperately for another subject other than murder.

VanEp said, "Relax and have a cup of coffee, Herman, you too Mr. Harris."

Mom had on one of her worried sick looks. My confused mind tried to give it a benign motive. Maybe she thought I should be in bed instead of having coffee or something. Deep down I knew something far more serious was the cause. Pop went over to the percolator on the stove and poured us both some coffee. I reached over, got three spoons of sugar, and added some cream. Mom always served real cream with her coffee, not the evaporated milk that some Navy wives used. Pop sat down. I dragged the extra chair over to the crowded table, plopped into it and looked vaguely at the two agents.

Mr. Hanson said, "Joe Carlson was found dead this morning over by the Hotel Del Coronado."

There it was, thump, right there. Carlson was dead. *I had murdered him.*

Pop's face registered surprise, then relief. "Well that means my son won't have to testify, doesn't it."

Mom just looked at him. Good old pop. He didn't give a rat's ass about Joe Carlson, just pleased his son got out of a tough and dangerous spot. A few disjoined thoughts ran through my head. Carlson's wrist spouting blood intermixed with my swinging the ashtray and images of Liz in bed all fused together. If I had been alert, my fear would have shown. It was still there, buried deep somewhere, but held down by my stupor. I just looked at Hanson and shook my head.

He went on, "It appears like suicide, but the body's location near the hotel pool is strange. A knife stuck in his wrist had hit an artery. He bled out right there by the pool."

Pop's neck started getting red. I watched the redness grow. Again, my mind was looking for some escape. Watching Pop's neck as his anger rose, I heard him say, "What the hell was he doing there. He was – was supposed to be in custody of his parents – not out of their sight. You said that was a condition of his bail." His voice rising, he stood and slapped the table with his open palm. Why? You guaranteed my son's safety."

He rarely got angry, but Pop could really blow up when he did. Now he let loose. Thank God for Pop. I hoped they'd focus on calming him down and forget me.

"We're sorry, Mr. Harris," Hanson said. "He apparently slipped out late at night. We're trying to figure out why he was over by the hotel. Why did he commit suicide there? Furthermore, there was no note," VanEp said.

"I bet he went looking for Herman, to prevent his testimony. Joe Carlson faced prison for a long time," Mom said.

"That's a possibility that we're considering, Mrs. Harris," Hanson answered.

Mom…please…just shut-up.

Then VanEp turned to me and said, "I understand from your mom that you were at the prom over at the hotel last night."

The hangover kept my answer brief.

"Yes."

"Did you see or hear anything that could help us?" VanEp said.

"Nothing out of the ordinary; maybe Joe's friends saw him at the prom," I said.

I tried to point them away from me.

"We're going to interview some of them. It appears that you won't be further involved Herman. Thank you for all your help in this. Without you, we couldn't have cracked this gang. I guess you'd like to get some sleep now. Did you enjoy the prom?"

God, it's over.

"Yes, very much," I said.

Pop got up and saw them to the door. I sat there for a minute then pulled myself up and told Mom I was gonna to hit the sack. She smiled and patted me on the back.

I slept until 2:00 pm, dreaming disjointed images of VanEp, Joe Carlson and Liz, intermingled with a wrist spouting blood. The aspirins hadn't helped much. My head still pounded.

Not long after I got up, the local TV station reported Joe Carlson's death. They had a short view of his father the Colonel and his weeping mother coming out of the morgue after verifying his identity. They called it an apparent suicide, but said the FBI was still investigating. They said Carlson was a key witness in the FBI's case against a Mexican drug gang. They didn't say anything about my scheduled testimony against him.

For the next several days, I minded my Ps and Qs as my mom used to say. I did my paper route and studied extra hard for finals. My nightmarish dreams eased only when Liz's face appeared, floating like an angel. The last day of school was Friday. I got my grades, two B pluses and the rest Bs. Saturday at noon I parked outside the church to wait for Liz. We hadn't talked since the prom. She came over to my car with a smile on her face that melted me. For a few minutes, I forgot all about Joe Carlson. We drove to the Rexall Drug Store and took a seat in our favorite booth.

Over a chocolate shake she said, "I had a talk with my mom about you."

"Huh, oh," I said. "You didn't tell her, did you?"

"No, no, I'd never do that. If I did, she'd probably never let me out of the house, or maybe even ship me off to a convent or something." Liz laughed. "She told me that I could see you once a week after religious school. She preferred that we didn't date other than that."

I'd been thinking of our situation, I told her, and I'd want her day and night, if we dated. Then she might accidentally get pregnant. I didn't see us considering

208

marriage or going off and eloping. I wouldn't be able to support her. I told her I still wanted to see her and maybe someday things would work out. I told her I had never developed a serious relationship before because I was simply too young, but she wasn't like other girls and I couldn't stop my feelings for her.

I didn't tell her Katie Gutierrez might have elicited the same response in me. Then a rush of guilt about Joe Carlson hit me. No one, including Liz could ever know.

She smiled and said, "I don't regret what we did. I need to get away from these religious hang-ups, but we better be careful when we play adult games. Let's just see each other for the shakes and maybe a date at the end of summer before I go off to college. My mom would be so relieved. She sees us together and worries. She's afraid that I'll elope or something."

The following week, the TV news reported that an autopsy on Joe Carlson concluded that someone fractured his skull before stabbing his wrist. The report further stated that the FBI had opened a case, considering it a homicide. The report didn't say what caused the fracture, just saying a blunt object caused it. I wondered if the ashtray still stood where I left it. The hotel probably emptied it several times since I swung it. I figured it unlikely that they would get my fingerprints off it, but I wasn't sure. I expected another visit from Mr. Hanson and Agent VanEp.

I went over the incident repeatedly in my mind trying to justify my actions. I used his own hand to stab his opposite wrist. Then when it spouted blood, I just left without seeking help. A jury would probably consider it murder. I could claim self-defense, but the incident would scare the hell out of Liz, ending our growing relationship. I admit that I felt too scared to come forward about it. My overwhelming rage for just that instant was inexplicable. I could never understand my actions that night. I knew with a shuddering reality that I was capable of murder.

24

Monday July 18, 1960

The two Coronado police officers came back to talk to me about two weeks after their first visit. Pop was calmer when they knocked on the door with the base legal officer, a young Lieutenant who looked only a couple years older than I did. The Lieutenant told Pop that the base CO requested that he cooperate. He stepped aside while the cops and Pop talked.

"We have the ashtray that bludgeoned Joe Harris before someone stabbed him with his own knife. We found some hair and skin from Joe Carlson's head on it." The first cop said.

He stood in our living room wearing a crisp khaki uniform short-sleeve shirt. A holstered gun hung on a black leather belt on his matching pants. He spread his legs and stiffened his back.

"Yea and you know that Carlson and his gang nearly murdered my son." Pop said.

"It's strictly a formality. The FBI suggested that we check fingerprints of people who knew Carlson for comparison to those on the ashtray. They believe that the Mexican drug gang killed him, but if they can match any fingerprints, they want to interview that person. If they get no matches from Carlson's friends or associates, they can concentrate on the gang alone."

"They would like to eliminate your son as having anything to do with the murder. Remember he attended the prom that night in the general area of the murder," the cop said.

My mind raced. Fearing that I would just blurt out my guilt at some point, I tried to listen calmly. The murder filled my mind. The two cops kept glancing at me as they talked. Probably thought I would bolt – a crazy thought. They couldn't know that I did it. I wanted to bolt anyway, but where would I go? They'd catch me. With my whole life on the line, I had to keep the murder secret.

The other cop held an inkpad and a fingerprint card in his hand. He moved toward me. I tried to look cool and eyed Mom and Pop. They looked concerned. I hoped my prints on the ashtray had been smudged or something. Pop must have read my mind.

"How many people touched that thing before and after the murder? How the hell can you get anything but smudged prints and what about all the hotel staff?" He said.

The second cop stood in front of me. "We probably can't find any match we could use in court. The thing stood out there three days before the autopsy revealed it had been used to hit Carlson, but you never know what might turn up."

I didn't say anything, just stood there like a dork. Pop never really consented and I hadn't said a thing, yet the cop grasped my hand and told me to extend my index finger. He rolled it on the pad and then on the card.

"It'll be easier if you don't tense up," he said.

Don't tense up. Shit, I was scared shitless.

"Just nervous, I guess."

....

Friday July 22, 1960

Studying and delivering papers never caused me trouble. Football caused it. Those first suspicions of the coach being paid off lead me to try to stop the drug selling in my school. It wasn't the parties or the chicks; it was football, the coach and marijuana. Why didn't I just let it go? I never understood my rage. My fear lead to some kind of uncontrollable rage. That's how I killed Joe Carlson. I could have stopped after I hit him, but some deep urge led me to stab him and then leave him there to die.

Now my whole future depended on this secret. Otherwise, it would have been a great summer. Liz's parents prevented me from seeing her much, but we still met on weekends. The beach parties and the surfing all made for a bitch'n summer. How many 17-year-old guys had it so good, living near the beach in an idyllic place? The fear - that was it, the pure fear of being caught drove me crazy day and night. Joe Carlson's death didn't bother me. The fact that I could kill didn't bother me. The uncontrollable rage that lived within me didn't bother me. It was being caught. That was it.

The cops had my fingerprints now. They would compare them to the prints on the ashtray, where there could be hundreds of prints. How many others had touched it? How long had it been out there before they confiscated it?

213

They must have a lot of smudged prints, maybe too many to find one that matched one of mine. I prayed that they wouldn't make the match. Praying that I not be caught for murder seemed wrong, but I did it anyway. It made me feel better, probably because of all that religion Mom drilled into me.

The cops took prints from some of Carlson's friends at school. Word circulated that they had paid some other visits. They also took prints from many of the hotel workers. I don't know how they selected them, probably all the Mexicans, thinking that they may have been part of the drug gang.

....

10 AM Tuesday July 26, 1960

I was about to head for the beach. The guys were there and the place rocked this time in the summer. Laurel and Hardy showed up at my house again. I gave them nicknames in my thoughts, degrading them, comparing them to those two hapless comics in the movies. The two cops scared me. Maybe they were just doing their jobs, but I sure thought they had it out for me, just me.

They knocked on the screen door. Our doorbell was on the blink and Navy Public Works would probably take forever to fix it. Those civilian workers moved slowly in the summer. Pop said they knew they couldn't be fired. The uniform Navy couldn't touch them and their union protected them. I'd put the whole Carlson thing out of my mind. Now here it was again, crashing into my life. *Crap.*

Mom answered the door. I just stood quietly in my bedroom, looking sideways out the window. I heard one,

214

the cop I called Laurel, say "We need to take Herman to the station for some questions."

After a silence, Mom answered, "Whatever for?"

I could picture her there at the door her face reddening with concern. I wished the whole thing would disappear. Why had I gotten into this? My heart thumped hard. *Stay cool, Mo.* They probably didn't have any evidence. I told myself that my fingerprints must have been smudged with dozens of others. How could they prove anything?

"We just need to ask some routine questions, Mrs. Harris. We're talking to everyone involved."

Mom started chirping then. In a high almost sing song voice, betraying her tension, she said, "My son wouldn't do anything like that, you know they tried to kill him don't you? Why do you keep coming back?"

I walked out of my room. "I guess I have to cooperate, Mom," I said.

I remembered the cop that I called Laurel. He manned the desk the time I tried to get the police to stop the drug dealing at school. I figured the whole department was just as dumb as him. I was damn scared, but I tried to think rationally. They weren't much as cops go, I told myself. The FBI guys had dropped me as a suspect, why couldn't the police let me alone?

I recalled Joe Carlson's kidney punch at the Christmas party. It reminded me of the rage I felt when I killed him. That little reverie eased my fear as I rode in the back of the cop cruiser to the station. Why didn't they just call and ask me to come down? No, they had to be big shot douche bags and make me ride in the back of the cruiser like a criminal or something. Laurel and Hardy weren't the right names for them. They both reminded me of *Barney Fife* on the *Andy Griffith Show* -idiots.

The station was less than a mile away. They parked right in front on Orange Avenue and paraded me in the front door. I figured it for intimidation – the whole thing – designed to scare the shit out of me. It did. I told myself that I had experience. After all, I had met with the FBI at their headquarters. These cops were rubes compared to them, I told myself, but I trembled inside, afraid that I'd blurt out something incriminating.

They ushered me into a small room, an interrogation room. I told them I had to take a leak. They told me to sit down and shut up. They had turned on the tough guy stuff. I didn't care. Let them think I had to take a piss. I didn't. That was just to con them. Their attitude pissed me off. That deep rage thing I harbored clicked on like a light. My fear turned to rage. They could question me all day, *fuck em*, I thought.

I had watched all the cop shows. "Am I under arrest? If not, I'm gonna just walk out of here. I don't like your attitude." I said.

The one I called Laurel just stretched and looked at me.

"Sit down wise ass."

I sat. The hard wooden chair pinched. A crack ran through the middle that opened and closed whenever I moved. *Crap*. It only made me madder. My fear evaporated.

"I don't have to take this. I know my rights," I said.

"Minors don't have rights, kid," The other douche bag cop said.

I didn't know if that was true or not.

"My Pop will go to the base legal officer. You can't just grab me at home without his permission."

"Your Mom didn't object," Hardy said.

I had just guessed about Pop's permission being needed. Now I figured I was on to something. They had picked a weekday when Pop worked; figuring Mom would be easier to deal with.

Hardy turned friendly. "Look kid we just need to question you, it's part of the routine. Just answer our questions and you can go home. Sorry we got off to a bad start. You can take a leak if you want. The head is just outside around the corner."

After scaring the shit out of me, now they tried the sweet approach figuring I'd be relieved and let my guard down. That pissed me off. The abrupt change from bad cop to good cop was horseshit, I figured. I had seen all that stuff on *77 Sunset Strip*.

"Fuck you."

Playing games – that's what I was doing with Sue and Larson. Playing detective seemed so natural after engineering a handoff of clinging Sue to horney Larson. If

BITCH'N

I had known it would lead to this; I'd have ignored the drug thugs, let someone else worry about them. It was no skin off my ass if half the kids in school ruined their lives with drugs. Fuck'em, that's what I should have done.

"That's not smart, swearing at us, son." Hardy said.

"And you're not smart pulling this good cop bad cop shit."

"You watch too much TV, kid. Look we know you helped the FBI get that drug gang. We also know Joe Carlson had a reason to go after you since you agreed to testify against him. We'll help you; it must have been self-defense or something. He came after you; you defended yourself, and you got a bit carried away. Isn't that how it happened?"

"I didn't have anything to do with Carlson's death. How could I? I was with Liz, my date."

They were too close to the truth. I fought to keep my voice level. The anger thing kept me together but the fear came back. God, don't blurt out anything, I thought. Had they talked to Liz, I wondered. Crap, they'll surely talk to her now. What if she tells them about me getting the cokes?

"Yea, yea, we talked to her. She said you two stayed together, but your friends said you and Liz stayed back at the hotel room while they went to parties. What went on there?"

"Ask Liz."

"She said you talked."

"The thing is Herman, Joe Carlson died by the pool at about the same time as you and Liz were "talking" at the hotel after the prom. Your friends tell us that they had already gone off to an after-party."

"What, ya think now that Liz helped me kill Carlson. I told you, I'd nothing to do with that." My anger was coming back. They had no proof of anything. I figured it all for a bluff.

"What do ya think, you're gonna get policemen of the year awards or something if you can pin this killing on me? I didn't have anything to do with it." I was shouting now.

"Go pick on somebody else."

Laurel moved in close to me now, turning on the heat.

"You little punk, we know exactly when you killed him. Your girlfriend admitted that you went out to get cokes. That took a half hour. That's when you killed him, isn't it."

I just stared at him. He had it right, guessed right. My fear and anger at a peak, I shook with emotion. I stood up, pushing my face right up to his.

"I didn't do it, asshole. You can't hold me, I'm going home."

Hardy put a calming hand on me. Anyway, I guess he thought it was calming.

"Help us out here, Mo. Isn't that what your friends call you? You've helped police in the past. Look how you helped the FBI."

"Get your hand off me. You're not a friend. I tried to report that drug dealing to you and you just brushed me off. That's why I went to the FBI."

"We can arrest you now, if we want to, and throw you in jail until you make bail. You wanna go through all that? Why don't we take a break here? You go use the head. I'll get you a coke and we can come back here and chat calmly. We're just trying to do our jobs here."

I went to the head. It was a one toilet little room with a sink. I put the lid down and sat. I figured that they were fishing. They had no case. That's why they hauled me in to interrogate me, to get some proof. God I wished I'd never snuck up to listen in on those two Mexicans at the beach party. I should have let Mulligan look out for himself.

I remembered that first date with Liz. Everything was cool then. I was on top of the world. Liz, she must have been very honest when they interviewed her. I couldn't blame her. The interview must have happened recently. She never mentioned it. It must have happened since Saturday, probably a day or two ago. She would have called me about it. The cops interviewed other kids, I knew. I figured that they didn't bare down on them like me – just courteous questioning, but me – they were trying to make me confess. They must have a strong suspicion…if they had one of my fingerprints on the ashtray – that could be it.

That ashtray must of been touched by a lot of people. Whatever they had must be smudged. I had to think about how to respond if they hit me with a matching fingerprint.

My mind raced. If I claimed to have touched it at some other time, they would know I just made that up. Then they'd bore in. No, the best thing was to deny everything. Never admit even touching the ashtray. Anything they had resembling my fingerprint must be a mistake – that's the way to handle it.

I stood up and looked into the mirror over the sink. I looked the same. The act of just looking at my reflection pulled me back from my anxious fear. They had nothing. As long as I denied killing Joe Carlson, they could do nothing. I looked at myself. I could tough it out. I opened the door and walked out acting cool.

Hardy handed me an open coke bottle. I waived it away.

"Naw, I don't want any. You can have it." Back in control, I sat in Laurel's chair, forcing one of the cops to sit in the pinching one.

"One of you guys can have that crappie chair, I'll take this one."

Hardy sat in the remaining good chair. Laurel stood. He moved close to me.

Whispering, he said, "We have your finger print on the ashtray."

I thought I had planned for that, but it hit me like a brick on the side of my head and a kick, low...low in the stomach. I just stared at Laurel, trying to recover...no...no...
I said, "Bullshit, it's not possible. I've never been near that ashtray."

BITCH'N

Hardy's calming voice said, "Now, now, think about it
Herman. Maybe it used to be at another location in the
hotel. You kids are always over there chasing around or
something. The hotel staff could've moved it to the pool
area since then."

He was trying to trap me, offering me an opportunity to lie.
They probably had proof already that the ashtray hadn't
moved. He was enticing me to lie.

"No, I don't smoke. I've never been near that ashtray."
Frowning, I stood up, infuriated. My anger at his attitude
overcame my terror.

Laurel moved in. "Come on Harris, we know you did it.
You picked up that ashtray when he was chasing you,
swung it and cracked his skull. Then you stabbed him with
his own knife."

"Bullshit, ask Liz."

Laurel raised his voice to a shout. He moved right up next
to me. The skinny shit I called Laurel acting the bad role,
"The blood musta spewed all over you. How the hell did
you get it off? You went to the hotel bathroom and
washed up after, didn't you."

"No, hell no."

"You punk, how'd ya stay cool after that. That's when you
got the two cokes and brought them up to Liz. You must
of been a wreck then. But she didn't say you acted any
different...must be love...is she covering up for you? That
makes her an accessory.

"We can haul her ass in here and interview her. What do ya think she'll say."

Hardy stepped in then. "Okay, okay now Herman we don't want to drag your girlfriend into this. As I said before, it must have been self-defense. You can tell us. We'll do everything we can to support you if you just tell us how it happened."

I just stared at him. I figured I'd just keep denying it. They couldn't prove anything. If they had proof, they would have arrested me already. They probably made up that shit about the fingerprint. Scared deep down, I felt the anger deeper, the same hard anger that came from a primitive place, and that anger told me - *Fuck'em.*

I heard a tap at the door. I head Pop's angry voice. He pushed open the door. The base Legal Officer stood there with him.

"What the hell are you doing with my son."

The Legal Officer spoke. "I'm Lieutenant James; I'm here representing the base commander. He is concerned that the family of one of his best Chiefs is being bothered. We've talked to the FBI. They say there is no real evidence of any significance."

"You jerks have some nerve showing up at my home and terrorizing my wife and hauling my son off to the police station. Who the hell do you think you are," Pop said.

Hardy was trying to calm things down. "No need to get upset, sir we just had some questions. We've questioned a lot of the kids about this."

"You didn't haul them off to the police station."

"We have a fingerprint." Laurel said.

The Lieutenant spoke. "The FBI did that examination. Smudged prints covered that ashtray. Just because a piece of a print looked like Mr. Harris' doesn't mean anything. You don't even know when that fingerprint got on it. You have no evidence whatsoever. This young man came forward on his own to report drugs in his school. He gets good grades and he plays sports. What, may I ask, makes you think he could do this?"

The Police Captain entered the room. "I'm sorry Mr. Harris our boys overstepped a bit here. My apologies Herman, you're free to go."

I felt like giving the two stooges Laurel and Hardy the finger, but that wouldn't look good after what the Legal Officer had said. I shut the hell up. My heart still pounded like crazy. I don't recall our ride home. We dropped the legal guy off in the parking lot. Mom hugged me as I walked in, tears in her eyes.

Pop went into the kitchen, pulled down a rarely used bottle of Jim Bean Whisky, poured out a couple inches in three glasses, handed me one, Mom one and took one himself.

"Some occasions call for a good shot of whisky. This is one of them." Pop had a way with words.

Neither the cops nor the FBI ever came back to visit. The news said nothing about the ashtray. I hung out with the guys and made a few beach parties. Just about every morning I hit the beach after my paper route, body surfing. That wore me out, kept me out of trouble and kept the image of a dying Joe Carlson in the recesses of my mind. I had no more fights with anyone. I met with Liz every Saturday.

Toward the end of August, I took Liz on one date that her parents sanctioned - a movie date. We expected her mom to watch the time like a hawk. Liz bounced excitedly while talking about her new dorm room at the University of San Diego. Nervous, she talked on and on as girls do. We left the movie a few minutes early and parked. Like a flash, we jumped in the back seat. I used my Trojans and she showed that she hadn't forgotten a thing.

After, I said. "Don't go off to college and forget me."

She promised not to forget, but said that the next few years would be a test. Then, if we still felt the same way, maybe we could see each other regularly. I pointed out that I turned 17 the previous month, the same age as her. She told me my age didn't matter. She promised to call me with her dorm phone number once she got settled. Would I really see her again, with sororities, college boys, and all that?

25

Early Summer 1962

I had been sitting on a bench near the hotel. I stood up and got a whiff of the sea. I walked toward the hotel pool area with thoughts and images flooding my mind. The Joe Carlson murder went unsolved. No one in the world knew about our silent struggle by the hotel pool. My decision to stab him with his own knife seemed irrelevant to the world or anything anymore, but I lived with it every day.

The pool area had changed since that night. Hotel renovations made the layout different. I glanced around, looking for the ashtray.

A vision flashed in my mind. The killer swung the ashtray viciously, not fearfully but viciously. He leaped on the shuddering Joe Carlson like a banshee and with super strength forced the knife wielding hand to stab Joe's own wrist. In my vision, I was no longer the killer but the observer of a crazed young man doing the deed.

I walked around the pool cool like; afraid I would see the old ashtray, afraid of my pounding anxiety erupting somehow to reveal me as a killer. I didn't see any ashtrays anywhere around the pool. I sat in one of the poolside lounge chairs then, and took stock. My heart's pounding, eased. I looked again at the image in my mind and this time the killer blurred out, kind of like the way a movie depicts a person in a dream. Like something that happened a long time ago, maybe even just a story of the past, not real anymore.

Would anyone benefit if the story came out - certainly, not the Carlson family. They moved away after his death. The Colonel quickly arranged a transfer. Joe Carlson was no saint. If no one discovered my secret, would it make any difference? I told myself no, and not to me for sure.

I got up, walked toward the beach, and turned right along the sidewalk promenade. The surf looked bitch'n. Timeless, it broke against the sand at this beach for thousands of years. It would continue to break over these sands for untold ages in the future, no matter what I did or had done.

I joined the guys on the beach, and then headed out to the water.

The waves rolled in, breaking just right - warm water and no red flags, cowabunga. I worked my way out to the biggest breakers. A large swell rose up. I turned toward the beach and swam in front of the swell. It steepened and caught hold of me. I straightened out and stiffened my body. Its power pushed the water around me. I rode it all the way into the foam on the shoreline.

Surfers on the Coronado beach, the ones with boards, used them as props to attract the girls. No one road boards with any skill on the waves. The typical crowd of Coronado High School privileged kids, some flailed about now in the surf, very rarely staying on their boards long enough to complete a ride. It was my Coronado, a safe place with good people, a good place to attend high school. I spotted my buddies lounging on the sand.

I stood up and shuffled over to join the guys.

Hampton McCarty had controlled his drinking enough to earn top grades. He was headed to Dartmouth College. Rich Levesque picked San Diego State. He wanted to study architecture. USC accepted Jon Jackman. He hoped to play football there. Larson Burke, like his old man, planned a career in the Navy. He was going to Annapolis. I planned to attend San Diego State's business school.

College deferments put off the draft for all of us. Larson of course, would make a life of the military. Sitting there in the sun, we had no fears for our future. There was that Cuban mess, but our new president JFK, seemed to have that under control. There were advisors in Vietnam, a remote exotic country somewhere in the Far East. With bright futures, none of us would have to go to war like our fathers. Hitler was long gone and Japan sold cheap toys in the US.

We lounged on the sand. Rich and Hampton had shades on so they could stare at the chicks. Jon didn't care if they noticed. Many of them smiled when he leered at them. Larson still a square, never wore shades or stared at the chicks. He had his day with Sue Pricey in his sophomore year. She had gone off to college and Larson went back to being square.

None of us had a steady girlfriend. Hampton's girl, who had gotten pregnant in our sophomore year, moved with her parents to a new duty station. She gave up the child for adoption. Hampton hadn't dated much after. Just a few casual dates and rolls in the sand with chicks at beach parties. Larson had some casual make-out sessions at beach parties but nothing serious. Anyway, he couldn't

A. J. Converse

get serious with any chick until he finished at Annapolis. It was the same thing for Rich, nothing serious.

Then there was Liz. I talked to her on the phone many times over the past two years and met her for shakes in my junior year summer. We had no more sex, although there was still desire when we saw each other. Some part of my mind still held on to her. The Joe Carlson thing had faded in my memory. Later in my junior year, VanEp had stopped by the house one morning after my paper route to tell me they closed the case. They figured the gang of Mexicans murdered Carlson to prevent his testifying against them. I never heard again from the Coronado Police.

Across the beach, I noticed none other than Stan Huffman and Del Webber walking on the sand toward us. Stan held a six-pack. They asked if they could sit with us.

"Sure, no problem," I said.

Stan said, "I just want you guys to know I'm sorry for giving you grief in your sophomore year."

Stan had lost his baby fat and looked more mature. He wasn't acting like a badass any more. Now a junior at Annapolis, he hoped to serve his country as a commissioned officer. He had become square, a lot like Larson in his mannerisms. He offered me a beer. I passed. I really didn't like beer that much. Rich and Hampton took one. Del, a junior at Berkley, where he majored in Chemistry, was engaged to some Berkley chick. They asked about the football team. I hadn't played since sophomore year.

Jon told them some of his exploits especially in our junior year when the team won the league championship. They were surprised that I didn't play after my sophomore year. I told them I was more interested in getting halfway decent grades and saving for college. My Pop had just retired and he and Mom bought a house in a new area called Mira Mesa. He had a job at a small ship repair company on the waterfront. He worked on Navy ships. He took some courses to get an adult school teaching credential. He wanted to teach in a junior college or something. I told Stan and Del that I'd help my parents pay for my college by working part time.

Del said, "You sound dedicated."

Then he stopped talking and just looked. Along the water line of the incoming tide walked five very hot looking chicks. The big five had returned. They headed our way.

"Now you guys aren't going to start a fight to impress us are you?" Jillian Hankins said.

She still looked terrific and today wore a light blue bikini.

We laughed.

They all sat down on big beach towels. As usual, I sat in the sand with a threadbare towel covering my legs to keep them from burning. Liz sat in the middle of the group of girls. Katie Gutierrez was obviously pregnant. Someone else had gotten to her.

Jill said, "We're all in town to give Katie a shower. She got married a few months ago. She's already starting a family."

A. J. Converse

Katie smiled shyly. I looked at her and winked. She looked away. They were all in a good mood and Sue Pricey pulled a bottle of red wine out of her beach bag along with some paper cups.

"Care to share?" Hampton asked.

Sue poured him a small cup and gave it to Larson. She didn't look at me. Larson grinned at her. Rich smiled his sarcastic little smile.

"Say, how about you girls going cruising with us," Rich said.

"Where would we sit in that old run down jalopy?" Jill asked.

"You could sit on our laps." Jon said.

Under his breath, Rich said, "Or, take turns in the..."

Jill said, "oh no!"

She jumped up and threw her wine on him. Everyone laughed, including Rich. The girls asked Stan and Del what they were up to. They told them and the girls were impressed. They asked about our plans and we told them. We also told them that we had pledged to meet on the beach here in Coronado every summer, no matter where we lived.

"Good luck with that," Jill said.

BITCH'N

Then they all got up and said goodbye. They were heading to the Mexican Village Restaurant to celebrate Katie's shower.

Liz hustled over to me and whispered, "I'm moving to an apartment this year with some girlfriends, Mo. Call me when you move on campus at San Diego State."

She handed me a piece of paper with her phone number. I watched them as they walked back across the sand toward Ocean Boulevard. A group of hot girls, the big five, my last view of them all together. Liz turned briefly and waived at me. I returned it and looked at her.

She still had the finest ass in Christendom.

I dragged my eyes away from Liz and looked out to sea. I noticed fresh white water churning about 25 yards out. A rip was developing.

A. J. Converse

Acknowledgements

I thank early readers of this story for their comments, critique and encouragement. They are my daughters Lisa Converse and Christina Van Camp, friends Lynn B., and Leslee R.

I also value all the improvements brought about by my read and critique group: Candice, Craig, Debby, Devon, Donna, George and Pam. Their suggestions and hints helped turn this story into a novel.

Made in the USA
Las Vegas, NV
04 February 2022

43088353R00128